A PHOENIX LORDS NOVEL

ASURMEN

HAND OF ASURYAN

by Gav Thorpe

BLACK LIBRARY

A BLACK LIBRARY PUBLICATION

First published in 2015.
This edition published in Great Britain in 2016 by
Black Library,
Games Workshop Ltd.,
Willow Road,
Nottingham, NG7 2WS, UK.

10 9 8 7 6 5 4 3 2 1

Produced by Games Workshop in Nottingham.
Cover illustration by Mike Daarken Lim.

A CIP record for this book is available from the British Library.

UK ISBN 13: 978 1 78496 267 8
US ISBN 13: 978 1 78496 268 5

See Black Library on the internet at

blacklibrary.com

Find out more about Games Workshop
and the world of Warhammer 40,000 at

games-workshop.com

Printed and bound by CPI Group (UK) Ltd, Croydon, CR0 4YY

It is the 41st millennium. For more than a hundred centuries the Emperor has sat immobile on the Golden Throne of Earth. He is the master of mankind by the will of the gods, and master of a million worlds by the might of his inexhaustible armies. He is a rotting carcass writhing invisibly with power from the Dark Age of Technology. He is the Carrion Lord of the Imperium for whom a thousand souls are sacrificed every day, so that he may never truly die.

Yet even in his deathless state, the Emperor continues his eternal vigilance. Mighty battlefleets cross the daemon-infested miasma of the warp, the only route between distant stars, their way lit by the Astronomican, the psychic manifestation of the Emperor's will. Vast armies give battle in His name on uncounted worlds. Greatest amongst his soldiers are the Adeptus Astartes, the Space Marines, bioengineered super-warriors. Their comrades in arms are legion: the Astra Militarum and countless planetary defence forces, the ever-vigilant Inquisition and the tech-priests of the Adeptus Mechanicus to name only a few. But for all their multitudes, they are barely enough to hold off the ever-present threat from aliens, heretics, mutants – and worse.

To be a man in such times is to be one amongst untold billions. It is to live in the cruellest and most bloody regime imaginable. These are the tales of those times. Forget the power of technology and science, for so much has been forgotten, never to be re-learned. Forget the promise of progress and understanding, for in the grim dark future there is only war. There is no peace amongst the stars, only an eternity of carnage and slaughter, and the laughter of thirsting gods.

1

The daemons' death-shouts reverberated around the ancient catacombs, filling the temple with grating cries. Asurmen's blade flared with psychic energy each time its edge parted body, limb or neck of his semi-corporeal foes. Monomolecular-edged discs streamed from his vambraces, slicing apart the red-skinned bloodletters that stood between him and his goal.

The last of the daemons fell as the legendary Phoenix Lord reached the threshold of the inner sanctum. Silence descended, broken only by the sound of Asurmen's boots on bare stone. The floor underfoot was quite plain, made of large, interlocking rectangular stone slabs. The walls were decorated with the faded, chipped paint of a mural. What had once been depicted could no longer be discerned, though Asurmen knew it from memory. The temple had been full of colour at its height, the frescos and friezes displaying scenes from the oldest eldar myths, many of them depictions from the War in Heaven.

At the centre of the hexagonal chamber was a pedestal as broad as his outstretched arms, waist-high, the top of which was carved with an intricate pattern of runes inlaid with bright crystals. The runes and gems had a dim inner light, creating six segments of blue, green, red, black, grey and white. At the centre of the pedestal sat a single globe, roughly the size of two fists together, swirling with white fog.

Another already waited there – a figure garbed in armour coloured like shifting flame stood beside the rubies embedded in the sanctum table. He held a firepike across his chest, the long barrel gleaming silvery-gold, matching the detailing on his wargear. In his other hand was a triangular-bladed axe, the air around its head distorted by the shimmer of heat. A demi-surcoat made of overlapping scales hung from his waist, matched by other dragonscale elements on the warsuit. His helm was flanked with broad projecting crests, casting a dark shadow across the shrine.

The air around the figure was hot, the temperature raised by the barely suppressed anger of the Phoenix Lord known as the Burning Lance.

'Fuegan,' said Asurmen, bowing his head in greeting as he took his place at the dais. 'Has that time come, the appointed hour when your call will bring us together for the final battle?'

The Burning Lance slowly shook his head.

'Not yet, shrine-father,' he replied. His voice was a rasp, each word clipped as though spat through gritted teeth. Despite his tone, Fuegan's pose was deferential to his teacher. 'The threads of the Rhana Dandra are gathering together but it is not yet time for the final battle.'

Asurmen accepted this without comment and looked around, finding reassurance in the familiarity of his surroundings. Nothing had changed here – nothing could change in a place that existed outside of reality. The ceiling was covered in a thin coating of iron artfully decorated with threads and beads of bronze. Depending upon where one stood, one saw a different face looking down, each of the six primary Aspects of Khaine, the Bloody-handed God.

The crystal runes glowed bright in front of Asurmen, dappling the ceiling with deep blue. In their light the Phoenix Lord saw above him a stern, lean face. Not cruel, but uncompromising. The visage of Khaine the Avenger, Asurmen's chosen Aspect.

Footsteps echoed along the halls and Asurmen turned his head to look at the next arrival. In came Maugan Ra, black-clad, his battle gear set with images of death, wrought with bones and skulls. For a moment it seemed as though moans and cries of despair followed in his wake, and then the silence of long aeons settled again.

The Harvester of Souls was armed with a shuriken cannon fitted with a scythe-like blade – the *maugetar*, slayer of countless foes. He inclined his head slightly in acknowledgement of Asurmen but deliberately made no motion towards Fuegan. As hot as Fuegan's temper was, Maugan Ra brought with him the chill of the tomb. He took up a position opposite the Fire Dragon, becoming a statue in his immobility. The crystals before him burst into black flame.

Next into the sanctum was Karandras, emerging from the shadows without a sound. He was clad in green armour, one hand engulfed by a gem-studded claw like that of a scorpion, a long tooth-edged chainblade in the other. Even Asurmen had trouble focusing on the darkness-clad Phoenix Lord, who seemed to disappear into the space between the glittering crystals, reappearing next to Fuegan. The two of them exchanged a brief glance.

'Well met, Shadow Hunter,' growled Fuegan as the emeralds set into place in front of the Striking Scorpion lit the shrine with their jade ghostfire.

'I hear the call and I answer,' Karandras replied quietly. He nodded to Maugan Ra. 'It seems but a moment since we last parted company, shrine-brother of Death.'

'We do not speak of our outer lives in this place,' Asurmen said sharply. Karandras recoiled at the rebuke, almost becoming invisible again as his rune faded into dullness.

'Apologies, shrine-father, I meant no discord.' His voice was a whisper in the gloom. 'I will speak no more of the outer world and the time beyond.'

Asurmen accepted the apology with a nod and beckoned Karandras to take his place properly.

'Your tempered manner has always been an inspiration, Hand of Asuryan.' So spoke Jain Zar, appearing at a doorway to Asurmen's right, the long crest of her high helm drifting behind her in a psychic breeze, like the tresses of a goddess. Her armour was the colour of bone, light against the darkness past the threshold. She carried a long glaive with a silver head and a bladed triskele hung at her hip. Three quick strides brought her fully into the chamber – every movement efficient, smooth and promising – a latent energy that could be violently released at any moment. 'May it guide us well on this momentous occasion.'

Jain Zar stood to Asurmen's right, within arm's reach of the dais. The runes of her Aspect glowed with a clear white.

They waited, sensing that one more was coming.

There was silence for some time before Baharroth appeared, the glittering metal feathers of his winged flight-pack furled like a cape around his arms and shoulders, his tri-barrelled lasblaster slung to one side. He moved to stand between Jain Zar and Maugan Ra, the flutter of his feather-crested helm the only sound. His rune became many colours, like a shaft of light through a prism, ever-changing.

'I feel the call,' Asurmen intoned, 'and I answer it. I come here, to the First Shrine, outside of space, beyond time. I seek guidance.'

He paused and looked at his companions. Maugan Ra and Fuegan were intent on the central globe; the others returned his brief look.

'It is rare that all are called together,' the Hand of Asuryan continued. He took a moment, regarding his former pupils with eyes both new and old. He could remember them all when they had first come to him, afraid, alone, seeking guidance even though they had not known it. It was near impossible to reconcile those memories with the mythical warriors that shared the shrine with him. His own journey was no less remarkable, he realised.

'Truly rare,' said Baharroth, his voice like the sigh of a breeze. 'My shrine-kin, take a moment to mark the occasion. Be of no doubt that we are each to return to the mortal world with sacred duties.'

'Do you question our dedication, Cry of the Wind?'

snapped Fuegan, looking at his shrine-brother. 'Always you speak as messenger, the doom-bearer, the wings upon which change is borne. What sky-whispers have you heard, tempest tamer, that we should know?'

'No more than you know already, wielder of the pure flame. The storm unleashed follows you like a curse, and it will do so until the Rhana Dandra. You cannot outrun it.'

'Why would I even try?' Fuegan laughed, but there was little humour in him.

'If it is not the End of All that brings us here, why did you summon us, Fuegan?' demanded Maugan Ra, his voice deep, the words rolling around the chamber.

'The fire of war burns bright, searing my thread upon the skein.' Fuegan's attention moved to Asurmen. 'I followed. I do not lead.'

'I followed also,' said Jain Zar. Even standing still the Storm of Silence seemed to be in motion, seized in a singular moment of inactivity. 'Loud was the cry across time and space that brought me here, issued from the lips of the banshee herself. A wail that doubtless brings death to many when I return.'

'It is the will of Asuryan,' said Karandras. The scorpion lord appeared to change position without moving. The simplest gesture came out of nowhere. Subtle movements in stance altered one pose to another seemingly without transition. 'The heavenly dream falls upon us once more.'

'Just so, shrine-son,' said Asurmen. 'Beneath ten thousand suns have we walked and fought. Timeless and endless is our quest, to bring peace to our people. No more are we living warriors, we have become ideas, memories of glories past and mistakes not to be repeated. We are the teacher and the lesson. Though we share this place now, we are but fantasy and myth, imagined in this place by the dream-wishes of a dead god, our spirits drawn from the realm of fact and reality. Scattered again we shall be when we leave, to such times we left behind when we answered the call. We will each see what we see and act as we will act, as we have done since the sundering of the Asurya.'

They all nodded their acquiescence and turned their eyes upon the great crystal at the centre of the shrine.

'Let us seek the vision of Asuryan,' commanded Asurmen.

Each Phoenix Lord placed a hand on their name-rune and the central sphere rose from its resting place and started to revolve silently. As it turned it formed a kaleidoscope, shedding multicoloured light on the sanctum's occupants.

The light pulsed gently and the walls of the shrine melted away. The six Phoenix Lords stood beneath a storm-wracked sky, red lightning lancing across purple thunderheads above. The rage of thwarted gods made the ground crack and the sky burn. All about the shrine was devastated, a blasted wilderness thronged with daemons from great lords to mindless beasts, held at bay by the rage of Khaine and the blessing of Asuryan.

But nothing outside the wall of power moved, not as seen from within the stasis. The legions of daemons were a frozen tableau, the blazing storm nothing more than a bright pattern across the heavens.

A moment from the distant past, locked away for all eternity by the power of Asuryan's Heart, the *Asurentesh* that lifted higher and higher from the altar-pedestal, streaming rainbow light down upon the shrine-family.

Asurmen felt his immortal gaze drawn further and further into the globe, until he was utterly lost within it. He saw the skein for a moment as the farseers witness it – a terrifying, impossible mesh of interlocking and overlapping fates. He saw his own thread, sapphire and vibrant, unbroken for an age. For a moment he saw the lives of the others branching out from the node of the shrine, but they fell away as the rest of the skein faded, leaving only a golden trail that drew Asurmen along until it plunged him into a living nightmare.

All is red, of fire and blood.

Screams tear the air and planets burn.

Two craftworlds, tendrils of darkness linking them together, dragging each other to destruction.

The sharp laughter of a thirsting god as it sups from the slaughter.

Ancient talons of stone, piercing a bleeding heart.

Ebon claws that break as a white flame of salvation erupts from that heart.

The shrine was dim when Asurmen was released from the vision, lit only by the ambience that had existed when he had arrived. The other Phoenix Lords were still in their places. The globe and runes were dull and lifeless. Asurmen lifted his hand from the pedestal and the others followed his lead. He felt a moment of disconnection, of spirits parting, leaving him feeling incredibly isolated. It was his usual state of mind and Asurmen was quick to master the sensation.

'We have seen what must be done, each to their destiny. We speak not of what the visions show us, for it is unwise to cross the threads of fate. Our spirits depart, to return to the world of mortals, at such times and in such places as we left, and in the mortal sphere our lives will meet again. Khaine is sundered once more.'

In the distance he heard fierce cries and closer at hand threatening whispers.

'Our daemonic besiegers draw fresh strength and so we must leave before they grow bold enough to dare our wrath.'

The Phoenix Lords departed, their armoured forms swiftly swallowed by the shadows outside the sanctum archways, footfalls dwindling into silence within moments as they passed from the First Shrine back through its hidden webway connections.

Karandras paused at the threshold and looked back, raising his claw in salute. Asurmen accepted the gesture of respect with a single nod.

And then Karandras was gone and Asurmen was alone. The baying of flesh hounds was becoming louder, the thunder of brass-shod juggernauts growing. The noise of whetstones shrieked in the darkness.

It was not wise to remain any longer, even for a Phoenix Lord. In the real universe he was functionally immortal, but the First Shrine was far from the real universe.

Asuryan had shown him his purpose. A wrong to be avenged. There was a war to end.

Blade at the ready, Asurmen stepped back into the darkness and the daemons attacked.

2

I should have brought more warriors, thought Asurmen.

The humans crawled over the ancient Jhitaar mausoleum like ants beneath a moonlit sky, clad in bulky environment suits and bulbous glass helmets. Large excavation machines were digging through the rubble, tossing aside columns and lintel stones as they delved into the subterranean city. Huge lamps blazed zones of stark light onto the brown stone.

The emergency webway breach behind the Phoenix Lord flickered as more of his followers arrived, dispersing quickly into squads led by their exarchs. In all, only two hundred and thirty-eight Dire Avengers from three nearby craftworlds had been able to answer the call of their spiritual leader. Jhitaar-space was almost uninhabited, after the scourge that had been the Fa'ade'en.

This close, even though the task force was on the surface, Asurmen and the other eldar could feel the presence of the Annihilator Shards beneath the rock. They were not far down. So close, in fact, that the humans must have discovered them already and were digging them free.

'We have to stop them!' Asurmen led the attack, emerging with his small host from the shadows of a toppled building to attack the humans closest to the centre of the tomb.

His vambraces spat a hail of death, the shurikens needing only to slash though the fabric of the humans' suits or shatter their helms to expose them to the deadly atmosphere. Made even clumsier by their protective wear, the soldiers around the edge of the dig site responded slowly. They had been watching their perimeter, not expecting a foe to materialise at the heart of their encampment.

'We have moments before they respond,' urged Asurmen as his squads fired their shuriken catapults, cutting down the red-suited figures between them and the central tomb complex. 'We might still succeed.'

Something emerged from one of the excavated levels, stomping up time-worn steps. It was far bigger than a human, its face a mass of pipes and respirator filters, eyes hidden behind goggles of smoked glass welded into its flesh. Steroid-inflated muscles churned as it lifted a huge rotary cannon into firing position.

The Dire Avengers scattered before the artificially mutated beast could fire, using walls and collapsed pillars for shelter. The sound of the cannon's discharge was a continuous roar that split the air as the ogre-beast slewed the weapon left and right, a torrent of shells shattering ancient masonry in a cloud of shards and dust.

Asurmen broke from cover as the half-human creature turned its gun away from the Phoenix Lord. Sporadic fire from other defenders sparked from the stone around him but he was too swift, the las-bolts streaming past. He was almost upon the creature before it even noticed his approach and started to swing its weapon towards him.

Asurmen leapt the last gap, his diresword glittering in his grasp as the point slashed across the bulging pipes that spewed from the monster's mouth and throat. He landed behind it and thrust his sword into its back, rupturing veins that spilled greenish, chemical-tainted blood. Oxygen hissed out of the damaged face-pump and the creature thrashed, unable to drop the weapon that had been melded to its forearm. Wild as it choked to death, the cannon-beast continued to fire, spraying shells into the air and across the tombs, cutting down humans and eldar in a burst that only ended when the ammunition hoppers on its back ran empty with a loud whine.

Not looking back to see the final death of the creature, Asurmen continued towards his goal. He leapt over piles of discarded soil and bricks and dodged around a litter of twisted foundation rods and the metal legs of the craneworks above. A few of the humans tried to bar his progress and were swiftly slain for their foolishness, either by a hail of shurikens or the edge of Asurmen's diresword.

He finally reached the main excavation and looked down into the pit that had been dug. Despite his supernatural gaze he could not make out much detail – just an inky blackness darker than the shadows that concealed the Shards.

Looking around, Asurmen saw the steps leading down into the antechamber of the Shard tomb. As he headed towards the stairwell he thought how typical it was of the humans to meddle with something so deadly, utterly ignorant of the doom they were bringing upon themselves and others.

It was still a mystery to the Phoenix Lord how the Fa'ade'en had found the Shards, for the Annihilator Obelisks had last been seen at the distant end of the galaxy, on the outskirts of the ancient eldar empire. But the artefacts of the Chaos gods had minds of their own, and an evil will to be discovered – none more so than the Shards. Even when the Annihilator Obelisks had been broken and the Shards scattered, it had not been enough. The fall had beset Asurmen's people and the final destruction of the Chaos weapons had never come about.

Taking the steps three at a time he descended into the depths, passing the glowing red globes of the humans' lights. It was not far down into the first chamber, adjoining the ground in which the Shards had impaled themselves a long time ago. He could feel the malevolence leaking from the alien things, trying to persuade him to free them.

How easily they must have turned the humans to their cause. Scavengers, picking over the remains of the Jhitaar core worlds, about to be consumed themselves.

The antechamber was alive with light, which came from no source but the arcane friezes that lined the walls. Asurmen could make no sense of the carved pictograms, but could see that they moved subtly, crowds of strange figurines coming together, closer and closer, raising their hands as if in praise.

A thunderous crash reverberated through the tomb, almost throwing Asurmen to the ground. He moved to the opening that led to the chamber of the Shards and watched in horror as the black wall beyond slid upwards.

The wakening minds of the Shards howled, echoing through the Phoenix Lord's thoughts. In moments the blackness had gone, leaving behind the harshly lit excavation. Standing on the lip of the deep abyss left by the Shards' exit, Asurmen looked up to see the jagged weapons rising against the sky, blotting out the stars with their shadow-wreathed forms.

And then blackness pulsed downwards, a ripple against the night sky.

The cranes evaporated, the scaffolding and girders melted. The humans had no time even to shout as the energy wave smashed into them. Asurmen threw himself backwards, but there was no eluding the monumental undulation of pure warp energy.

It burst through the opening like water through a breached dam, picking up Asurmen to hurl him across the antechamber. He slammed into the ceiling and then the far wall, tossed around and spun about as the Shards' energy whirled about the room in a vortex.

And all went black as life left him, his final thought a lament at his failure.

3

We are betrayed.

The thought entered Neridiath's mind the moment she felt a surge of energy washing over them – a sensor feedback from the human ship raising its defensive shields. It made her skin prickle with apprehension. The other vessel had not slowed. In fact, it was increasing speed even as Neridiath had been slowing the momentum of the *Joyous Venture*.

Afraid.

The thought was not hers but it was in her mind all the same. It emerged from the rush of concern that flooded the starship's psychic matrix, directed at Neridiath through the babble of emotions from the rest of the fourteen-strong crew.

'Their weapons are powering up.' This was from Kaydaryal. She sat on Neridiath's left, wholly interfaced with the sensor screen of the *Joyous Venture*.

I need to concentrate. We'll be safe.

Neridiath's subconscious had been guiding the ship but it was time to take direct action. She allowed the rest of her thoughts to be swallowed by the matrix: one moment she was a flesh-and-blood creature with two arms, two legs and a head, the next she was a twin-sailed tradeship sustained by energy drawn from the nearby star. From the solar sails the power coursed through her, fuelling the matrix and engines, flowing through scanning blisters and life-support domes. The rest of the crew were as much a part of the ship as Neridiath, fourteen minds separate but interlinked.

Through Kaydaryal's eyes she saw the human ship turning, bringing its broadside weapons to bear. It seemed a lazy manoeuvre, punctuated with the blast of retro-engines, brutal and slow. She was already adjusting the trim of the sails and manipulating the gravity drive to turn the *Joyous Venture* away from the humans, pushing the nose down relative to the plane formed by the two ships, turning like a breaching whale.

'Where are you going?' demanded Faelanthil, manning the weapons array. 'You are turning our lance arrays away from the enemy.'

'We are not fighting,' she replied tersely. 'Taerathu, why are the holofields not activated?'

'Redirecting energy from the core matrix now.' Taerathu sat on Neridiath's right but her words came through the ship's systems, an echo of the voice that Neridiath's ears were hearing. She tried to block out the distraction as the *Joyous Venture* continued to dive and roll, heading for a course that would take them under and astern of the human vessel.

'Why are we running?' Faelanthil's question was

underscored by a hot slash of energy build-up in the lances. 'We should disable their engines, destroy their life support and when they have all died of exposure we take what they owe us.'

Fael has a point, added Laurennin, the merchant that had commissioned Neridiath's ship for the deal with the humans. She could feel that he was currently in the starboard living quarters, helping himself to a goblet of restorative tonic. *Why should we sacrifice our part of the bargain because of bad faith by the humans?*

Neridiath felt a flutter of dislocation as the holofields activated, scattering the visible signature of the merchant vessel and casting scan-echoes across the nearby void.

'I am not fighting.' Neridiath started turning the *Joyous Venture* back upon its previous course as the humans clumsily fired attitude thrusters to compensate for the evasive manoeuvres of the eldar vessel. 'You want to become pirates, find another ship.'

We have come all of this way, insisted Laurennin, *it would be unfortunate to return with nothing to show for our efforts. Certainly not for the lives of a few human ill-faiths. I would have to make my displeasure known to others.*

'Do whatever you feel necessary, Laurennin. I can live without your praises.'

And your crew, will they stay with you?

'That is a decision I leave to them at the end of every voyage. Now, allow me to concentrate on getting us away from here intact.'

As the *Joyous Venture* raced towards the turning human ship it became obvious that Laurennin's 'contact' was not a merchant at all. The human vessel bristled with weapon systems, its scanners far more powerful than anything the eldar tradeship had encountered before. The humans' crude arrays lashed out tracing lasers and radiation waves in an effort to locate their foe.

'It was a trap all along,' said Taerathu.

'Just as well we did not try to fight,' said Neridiath. 'They have us heavily outmatched in firepower.'

'They cannot hit what they cannot see,' insisted Faelanthil. 'Move in behind them and our forward lance will soon disable their shields and engines.'

'You have a great deal of faith to trust all of our lives to the effectiveness of our holofields and the paucity of their scanning capability. We already have to run the risk of them opening fire just to get past. I see no reason to attack.'

If you wish to run away, why are we moving towards them? asked Laurennin.

'The time any of you have the slightest notion how a grav-drive works or understand the forces that act upon a starship when turning at high speed is the time that any of you are welcome to come up here and steer instead. Until then, be quiet!'

Her words were accompanied by a mental imperative that shut down the communications system across the ship. Neridiath could still feel the assortment of resentment, anger, fear and confusion amongst the crew and passengers but she no longer had to listen to it, leaving her free to focus on the threat at hand.

The humans had timed their attack well, and despite the derision of Faelanthil and others like him, the other vessel was military in purpose, unlike the *Joyous Venture*. As it was, the *Joyous Venture* would have to brave the guns of the enemy in order to slip away.

After a few moments she missed the arguing. It had distracted her from the fear. She felt the full weight of the situation pressing down on her as she glided across the vacuum of space towards the human ship, trusting her survival to a complex battery of sensory displacement fields. They faced firepower that could cripple them with a single salvo, and there was no choice but to avoid a prolonged contact.

That was the reasoning Neridiath used to justify a decision made by instinct. Fear was leading her, but she did not try to fight it. The fear was better than the alternatives.

The sensor feed from Taerathu showed the enemy scans grasping and flailing like hands across the void, seeking something to latch onto. It was tempting to try to steer between the greatest concentrations and pulses of energy but Neridiath knew that speed was their best defence. The faster the *Joyous Venture* moved, the greater the diffraction by the holofields and the less time they would be exposed overall.

Neridiath made a small adjustment, trimming the sail for maximum exposure to the local star, siphoning off a little more precious energy to direct through the grav-engines.

A tickling sensation, subtle at first, grew in strength, and soon become an unpleasant ache at the back of her head. She was already riding a dangerous line between the amount of energy coming in and the amount expended by the gravity engines. If she made a mistake in attitude and approach there would be a catastrophic power drain, or worse, which would leave them drifting and exposed.

The sensation of a bubble bursting enveloped her as Kaydaryal impelled the communications matrix back online, overriding her order with a burst of willpower fuelled by panic.

'They have us locked in their sights!' she warned.

'Too late,' Neridiath replied.

The *Joyous Venture* slipped under the human ship, passing through an exhaust wash of radiation and plasma spewed from its crude thrusters, scything through the mesh of tracer lasers and radio waves trying to pinpoint the eldar position. Neridiath levelled out the ship's course as the human vessel continued turning laboriously astern, trying to bring its main weapons into firing position.

Slipping out of the energy wake of the other ship, the *Joyous Venture* headed straight towards the star, sails drawing in the solar wind as a suffocating person might heave in a massive draught of breath. Not only did the stream of energised particles flood into the grav-engines, it washed over the eldar ship, the back-scatter blinding the humans' sensors.

Returning partially to her body, Neridiath let out a breath she did not know she had been holding. Almost immediately there was a timid mental contact.

Safe?

Yes, we are safe.

Neridiath stepped out onto the oval landing at the top of a stair that led down into the habitation decks of the *Joyous Venture*. At the bottom she stopped by the first door – her chambers – and the portal opened like a dilating iris, disappearing into the smooth walls.

Stepping inside, Neridiath moved quickly through the communal first room, furnished with several chairs and couches, arranged carefully between numerous low tables and shelves packed with hundreds of knick-knacks and mementos from her travels. There were gems both uncut and fashioned, nuggets and ingots of strange elements alloys, crude statues, and busts and charms from three dozen different pre-civilisation species along with amulets, jewellery, holy icons and figurines from a dozen thought to have reached the minimum level of technology and culture to be deemed worthy of formal approach.

None of her prized souvenirs attracted Neridiath's attention; she headed directly for the smaller of the two sleeping cabins. The door was sealed but petalled open at her command. Manyia stood by her table, still a little uncertain on her legs, and turned a wide-eyed look towards the door as her mother entered.

Happiness!

Her daughter's psychic surge of pleasure was almost overwhelming and Neridiath responded in kind, enveloping her child with warmth and love. She took up Manyia in her arms, replicating with contact what she broadcast with her thoughts. Manyia pulled away slightly and delivered an admonishing look to her mother.

Afraid. Bad people.

'Not any more,' Neridiath assured her daughter.

4

A detonation made Farseer Hylandris look up from his work. His thick robes were already dirtied by dust from the ceiling, the ancient plaster deteriorating further as more shells pounded the surface some distance above. The gems that studded Hylandris's ghosthelm were smeared with the same, as were the skintight worksuits of the twenty eldar that had laboured for the past three turns of the world to unearth the sealed doors that confronted the farseer. All eyes, hidden behind mirrored blast-visors, were on Hylandris as he attended to the circular rune-wheel they had excavated next to the massive gates.

Another shell showered more debris from the half-collapsed ceiling. The explosions were getting closer, which meant that the Chaos-corrupted humans were also getting closer to the *Ankathalamon*'s resting place, penetrating deeper into the City of Spires. Hylandris steadied his thoughts, studying the intricate pattern of gems and runes and the geometric shapes interlinking them.

He ran through all the possible combination patterns and ciphers he knew, from the Twelve Keys of Heredorith, through the hexopulent algorithms of the Bethannis quartet, to the constellation-memes of Pathedesian. None of them seemed to fit the interlocking runestone plates that formed the activation panel of the last portal to the *Ankathalamon*'s vault.

Farseer, the enemy are massing for attack on our right flank, through the Park of Winter's Thief. If we remain longer we will be surrounded.

The words of Nymuyrisan reached Hylandris without any mechanical aid. It came to him with a slight repeat – the thought-echo from the wraithknight pilot's dead twin whose soul was encased within the spirit stones of the massive war engine's body. When Nymuyrisan sent a psychic message, his brother Jarithuran could be felt lingering on the edge of the pilot's consciousness.

Counter-attack! Hylandris's frustration with the rune-disc lent extra venom to his thoughts. *We have already lost several warriors and machines sealing the entrances to the lower levels – we do not have the firepower or numbers to retake the city if we surrender our grip. Coordinate with the* Patient Lightning *for a strike from orbit.*

If we continue to push further from Niessis, we might be cut off from the webway portal. We will be stranded here.

Not while the Patient Lightning *continues to dominate in orbit.*

Tynarin has reported detecting several enemy ships that will arrive within twenty more planetary rotations.

Twenty days is more than enough time to break this code

and retrieve the Ankathalamon. *Remember, Nymuyrisan, if we fail here our craftworld is doomed.*

As you wish, farseer.

Hylandris dismissed the concerns of the wraithknight pilot and returned his attention to the rune panel. There was certainly a base-six code, perhaps one of the Triumvirate of Asuryan that was so common in the days before the Fall.

Lost in his contemplations, the farseer paid no heed to the communications relating to the ongoing battle above ground, so it came as some surprise when his thought processes were interrupted by a panicked intrusion from Tynarin, commander of the battleship *Patient Lightning*.

We are under attack! The mon-keigh have managed to activate several defence platforms we thought defunct. Anti-ship torpedoes are closing on us at speed.

Shoot them down or evade them, Hylandris replied irritably, wondering why this was a matter for his attention. *Must I tell you how to do everything?*

There is no time, farseer. I must enter the upper atmosphere and hope that the missiles burn up before they strike us. We will suffer damage, but it is better than the alternatives. If we are destroyed, the surface webway gate is your only exit. I am sending a web-bound distress call back to the craftworld, but it may be some time before help arrives.

As though to spite Hylandris's earlier decision, he heard on the communicator that his forces were being driven back towards the vault-temple, losing their hold on the gateway by which they had come to Escatharinesh. In a little under half a day their position had changed from dominant to precarious.

Nymuyrisan, what is happening?

We cannot engage in prolonged conflict, their numbers are too great, farseer. Better that we withdraw to the vault building and secure our line, and recapture the webgate when we are ready.

Entering the atmosphere now, farseer, reported Tynarin. *Heat dampeners are coping... Surface abrasion starting to take its toll... Isha weeps! We have heat flare across the dorsal system, losing trim and manoeuvring. All three pilots showing signs of feedback delirium.*

What does that mean? demanded Hylandris. *Tell me what is happening up there.*

We will have to conduct a controlled descent, farseer.

You are crashing?

Crash-landing. Hopefully.

Hylandris could feel waves of worry flooding from his companions, which he countered with a psychic pulse of reassurance.

There is no need to be afraid, he told them. *The way ahead may be painful but we will emerge victorious. I guarantee it. I have foreseen our success here, have I not?*

5

Light.

Stark sunlight.

Asurmen did not need to blink, had no means to do so, but he did the mental equivalent as he reviewed his situation.

He was still in the Tomb of the Jhitaar. He could see the markings on the wall. Dull, unmoving. The light was streaming into the chamber from a breached ceiling. He turned his head and saw a black-armoured figure lying lifelessly next to him. The last memories of the eldar echoed away inside Asurmen's spirit and a name: Tuathanem Ulthrander Naeith. A Black Guardian of Ulthwé. She had been following the Path of Restraint when not fighting in the militia of her craftworld. The last vestiges of her spirit drifted away into nothing and all that she had been and might be became Asurmen instead.

Her companions had retreated to the grav-nets

dropped through the hole in the roof and more figures were silhouetted against the bright sky beyond.

'She has found peace,' Asurmen assured them as he sat up. His diresword was on the floor where it had fallen from his dead grasp. He twitched his fingers. The weapon moved into his grip. The pommel and blade flared into life, recognising the Phoenix Lord's touch.

He had become accustomed to the glare from the hole and Asurmen realised there were streaks of red and white criss-crossing the visible patch of sky: laser fire.

'A battle? Against whom?'

'The Jhitaar.'

The voice that replied was quiet and even and came from Asurmen's left. He sensed old power, great wisdom and the weight of eternity emanating from the figure as he turned in the direction of the sound.

The farseer was dressed in a maroon robe beneath an open mantle of black embroidered with golden runes. He wore a ghosthelm, his features concealed, and in his right hand he held a staff of crystallised blue wraithbone, studded with spirit stones. A bared Witchblade gleamed in his left.

Incredible psychic potency and the presence of Black Guardians of Ulthwé made it easy to know the farseer's identity, even if Asurmen had not met him a score of times and more in previous lives.

'Eldrad.' Asurmen pushed himself to his feet and thought on the farseer's reply. 'The Jhitaar were driven back by the People of the Shards. How have they returned?'

'You have been here quite some time, Hand of Asuryan,' said Eldrad Ulthran, chief of craftworld Ulthwé's seer council and the greatest prophetic psyker the eldar possessed. 'A quarter of an arc by the reckoning of my people has passed since the Jhitaar returned to their core systems.'

'A quarter of an arc?' Asurmen made a quick calculation based on the trajectory of Ulthwé's movements. 'This world has orbited its star more than seven hundred times while I awaited resurrection!'

'Indeed. Rest assured that your awakening is timely. I was brought here by a vision, a waking dream that came to me as I studied the skein of possible futures. I did not know why, but it steered me towards the burial grounds of the Jhitaar. I thought perhaps some remnant of the Fa'ade'en war machine or civilisation remained.'

'It did,' Asurmen said grimly, moving towards the portal stones beyond the hole made by the eldar of Ulthwé. 'Three shards of an Annihilator Obelisk. The humans found them and woke them up. I tried to prevent it. I'm sorry, I was too late.'

'Why do you direct your apology towards me?'

'I was meant to see them destroyed. Asuryan... A vision I was given... The shard-ships are linked to the Rhana Dandra and the destruction of Ulthwé in some fashion.'

The farseer accepted this with a calm nod.

'As powerful as they may be, three Annihilator Shards are no match for the fleet and defences of a major craftworld such as Ulthwé. What danger they pose is minimal.'

'You are wrong, which cannot often be said,' Asurmen assured the seer. 'I know. I have seen what will happen. I was too late.'

'How can you see such a thing when I have not?' Eldrad scoffed at the idea. 'Not even with all the seers of the galaxy would I be able to pierce the veil that is the storm of the Rhana Dandra. I know that you are constantly drawn to unhappier fates and great moments in history. When countless lives entwine and hang in the balance, nodes of invisible futures, that is where you will be. It is the doom of the Asuryata, but all is not lost.'

'You have it wrong. Asuryan himself guides his Asuryata, you know that. We do not follow fate, it follows us. These nodes of invisible futures do not draw us, we are the nodes. The skein bends to our presence. The fates of all others may be hidden from me, but my own is as clear as crystal. I do not see the means, but the Shards are linked to the loss of Ulthwé.' Asurmen considered the possibilities. 'Perhaps they reunite with their core and others, and a full Obelisk is restored?'

'That would be... troubling. But let us not speculate too much. There are other means.'

Three pouches at Eldrad's belt opened of their own accord and a small constellation of wraithbone rune-shapes drifted into the air from within, each unique, circling about Eldrad and making orbits with each other. Asurmen sensed the Staff of Ulthramar vibrating gently in the farseer's grasp, a permanent link through the eternal matrix, joining Eldrad to the immense power of Ulthwé's infinity circuit many light years away.

The lenses of the farseer's ghosthelm gleamed gold with psychic energy.

'The oft-cried lament of our people since the Fall, "I was too late." Let us see what the future holds, Hand of Asuryan.'

'Tell me, how do we prevent this disaster?' Asurmen said. 'If there is any way that I can set right this course, I will do it.'

6

'Neridiath, could you come up to the control pod?' Kaydaryal's voice conveyed her uncertainty even before the emotion came to Neridiath across the ship's matrix. The other crew members felt it too and there was a gentle backwash of concern which coaxed an explanation from Kaydaryal. 'I'm picking up another ship close by in the webway, that's all.'

Manyia was sleeping, suspended in her grav-net, a fluffy gyrinx doll clutched across her chest. Checking her daughter's spirit stone pendant was secure around her neck, Neridiath gave Manyia a light kiss on the cheek before making her way up to join Kaydaryal.

Slipping into the steering cradle felt like returning to a loving companion, and Neridiath savoured the moment as its fronds enveloped her, drawing her into a gentle but firm embrace. She let her mind contact Kaydaryal's sensor banks, sharing her thoughts for a moment.

The webway flowed around them, streaming past as

a tunnel of energy, though more accurately it was the *Joyous Venture* that was moving, not the webway. The psychic matrix spread out past the skin of the ship, sending tendrils into the fabric of the webway itself like an anti-gravitic monoshuttle gripping its rail with electromagnetism – connecting but not quite touching. The *Joyous Venture* drew in power along this contact and simultaneously used the pulses of psychic energy to propel itself along the semi-ethereal route of the webway.

Some distance behind but gaining on them was another spark of power. Seeing it only from a tangent, Neridiath did not share the intimate connection that Kaydaryal had, nor did she share her concern.

'Another ship, as you said. I see no reason to adjust our course. Why are you so alarmed by its presence?'

Kaydaryal pulled herself out of her sensor-trance and looked at Neridiath, her silvery eyes intent.

'We are not close to the craftworld, and this is not a highly travelled trade route, so any encounter is unlikely. Also, the speed of the other vessel is something to behold. Almost twice as fast as we are travelling.'

'Twice as fast?' The *Joyous Venture* was no sun-racer, but that was an impressive feat. 'So, they're in a hurry. What else?'

'Battle-intent. The fabric of the webway is rippling with foreboding, a bow wave from that other ship. When it's closer, you'll be able to feel it too, the Khaine-lust. There are warriors on board.'

Acknowledging Kaydaryal's fear with a reassuring smile, Neridiath checked once more that all was well with Manyia – the child was still fast asleep – and allowed herself to be drawn into the piloting systems. As she did every time, she felt the thrill of exchanging frail, mortal limbs for the star-spanning power of a spaceship. The moment she was wholly interfaced with the engines and manoeuvring systems she detected a faint quiver of the war-like intent that Kaydaryal had mentioned, entering her thoughts as feedback from the webway structure itself.

She increased the energy output and took direct control of the ship's navigation. She eased up the grip of the psychic matrix, giving them less traction, which increased their speed but reduced manoeuvrability. Letting her thoughts flow ahead, she spied a secondary tunnel branching off the main webway passage they were following. A partial map of the nearby star systems and webway gates flickered across her synapses in an instant, identifying the junction as the branching point towards the Seraishamath System. Dead worlds, and beyond them a long journey to the next star.

Neridiath slowed again, preparing for the turn, feeling the ship behind them getting closer and closer as she did so. The shorter the distance between the two vessels, the more she could feel the scent of Khaine emanating from the other craft. It started to slow also, preparing to follow them around the curve into the sub-passage.

'What sort of ship is it?' she asked.

'Small, maybe a handful of crew at most. Craftworld-built, not Commorraghans. Possibly outcasts, so that doesn't mean we're safe. One weapons array, dorsal- and keel-linked lances.'

Another presence intruded on their discussion as Fael interfaced with the *Joyous Venture*'s lance control systems.

'In case they follow us out into mortal space,' he said, sensing Neridiath's disapproval and pre-empting the sharp remark that had come to mind. 'Better to be ready than sorry.'

Neridiath ignored him, determined that it would not come to a fight. She slowed the ship for the coming turn, letting the other ship get even closer, within extreme weapons range. Then she accelerated again, as though she had changed her mind and was going to outpace the other ship in the larger passageway.

'Only one aboard,' Kaydaryal said with some surprise. 'Vaul's hammer, but they make a big dent in the webway. A major psychic well on that ship, no wonder they can go so fast, channelling the traction energy directly through the pilot!'

The pursuing ship did not power up its weapons, but it did accelerate again, responding in an instant to Neridiath's manoeuvres.

'We'll be overhauled soon if we don't do something,' said Fael.

'Already ahead of you,' snapped Neridiath.

They were about to pass the exit to the sub-branch when Neridiath threw all of the psychic matrix into the flank of the *Joyous Venture*, effectively turning the left side of the ship into a massive ether-anchor. Only she felt the terrible wrenching of competing energies as impetus and psychic friction fought against each other, throwing a flare of immaterial sparks as the warp-grasp of the psychic matrix tried to snap away from the webway wall. For the others, inertia dampeners and the vessel's artificial gravity nullified any physical sensation the dramatic manoeuvre might have inflicted.

Neridiath threw all of her thought through the turn, hurling the energy from the inside curve to the outside wall, turning the power from a brake into a huge booster, slinging the *Joyous Venture* into the side-tunnel at full speed. It was almost too fast and the starboard stabilising wing came perilously close to impeding the psychic connection, but Neridiath managed the energy flow just in time, restoring the equilibrium through the ship just as it was about to power itself sideways into the immaterial wall of the webway.

The pilot shunted her thoughts across into Kaydaryal's systems for an instant, just in time to see the other ship perform an outrageous turn and loop, running upwards and across the outside of the junction before twisting through its own psychic matrix to follow after the *Joyous Venture* with no loss of momentum at all.

'Kurnus's blood!' hissed Kaydaryal.

'If I tried that manoeuvre, I'd turn my mind inside out,' Neridiath said in hushed awe.

'Shall I power up the lances?' asked Fael. 'I don't think we can give them the slip.'

The moment Fael mentioned weapons the webway shuddered slightly, his thoughts of possible conflict intermingling with the warlike presence emanating from their pursuer.

'No!' Neridiath told him, easing out her thoughts into the matrix engines to slow their progress. 'If they want to contact us so much, let's hear what they have to say.'

She guided the slowing starship towards a bay-like blister nestling in the roof of the webway sub-branch. It had been created to allow smaller ships to let a much larger vessel pass in the confines of the duct, but it suited equally well as a temporary berth. Warp grapples secured the *Joyous Venture* a safe distance from the fabric of the webway as Neridiath powered down the navigational engines. The other ship bled off momentum with a series of dramatic spirals around the webway tunnel, finally detaching from the webway wall to glide into position inverted beneath the *Joyous Venture* so that their docking portals could lock on to each other.

'Let's see who our visitor is,' said Neridiath as she slipped from the descending pilot cradle.

The others met her at the docking gate, in a chamber barely large enough to hold all of them. A hiss heralded the sealing of the two ships' environmental fields and with a puff of breeze from equalising air pressure the external door opened.

At the threshold stood a tall figure clad in layers of blue armour, his head encased in a high helm of red, with a white and black crest. His gauntlets merged with heavy vambraces along his forearms, each fitted with the barrel of a shuriken weapon. Gems of many colours glittered all across the ornate armour, filled with an energy of their own.

It was not the weapons or the armour that shocked Neridiath so strongly but the aura of death and ancient power that surrounded the warrior. The small room quickly filled with a sense of trapped energy, of terrifying violent potential held at bay behind a wall of pure willpower.

The warrior stepped aboard and the whole matrix thrummed with his presence. At the back of her mind Neridiath felt Manyia stir, her infantile enquiry puncturing the horrific miasma that surrounded the stranger.

New Person. Friend?

When the visitor spoke, it was with soft, mellifluous tones.

'I am the Hand of Asuryan and I need you. The future of the eldar depends upon it.'

7

The descent of the *Patient Lightning* left a scar across Niessis, the heat of its crash and the shockwave turning much of the abandoned eldar city to ruins. Linked by a thousand bridges across more than a hundred towering rock pillars and plateaus, the sky-city became a tomb for thousands of the Chaos gods' vile worshippers. The fortunate ones were incinerated alive but many were buried by the collapse of sandstone towers or plunged to their deaths when bridges crumbled beneath their feet. The lower levels of the sky-columns were wreathed in fumes from destroyed troop carriers and crude tanks that had plummeted to the ground, their tangled remains piled where they had fallen.

From high in the pilaster that topped the Tower of the Vault, Hylandris surveyed the aftermath. Towards the sunset a pall of black smoke hung over the forest that covered much of the land beneath the city. A hump of pale yellow and green marked the final resting place of the downed battleship, just visible beyond the column of black that polluted the magenta sky of Escatharinesh. Fortunately the prevailing wind, funnelled from the poles by an ever-narrowing series of valleys, was driving the forest fire away from the crash site.

'Tynarin did well to steer clear of the Vault Tower,' Hylandris told his companion, the warlock Zarathuin. The farseer pointed to a column of lights and smudge of exhaust smoke trailing along the main highway through the forest towards the battleship. 'The scavengers gather but they will find a beast ready to fight rather than some carcass to be stripped. At least this has distracted them from Niessis and we will be able to continue our work unmolested for a few days.'

'How can you be so dismissive of this disaster?' asked Zarathuin, alabaster skin creasing into a frown. 'You act as though all is proceeding as you have foreseen. It is not! You did not warn Tynarin of the attack in orbit, and I certainly do not recall you saying anything about being stranded on this moon surrounded by wild Chaos-tainted humans!'

Hylandris gestured for Zarathuin to follow as he headed towards the winding stair that led down into the bowels of the massive rock spire that had been carved into the Vault Tower by ancient hands. The warlock kept pace with him, his disapproval as tangible to the farseer as the protective aura of the rune armour that pulsed in time to Zarathuin's heartbeat.

'There have been setbacks, but the skein has not been significantly changed,' Hylandris said as they descended the steps. 'We will remove the *Ankathalamon* from its hiding place and ensure that the humans do not discover and activate it. These Chaos savages will survive long enough to halt Ulthwé's task force in Nerashemanthi-ash. For once it is the destination and not the journey that is important.'

'One can easily trip if one's eyes are forever on the hori-zon,' the warlock retorted. Hylandris always detected a hint of suspicion and jealousy from his far older compan-ion. Zarathuin put on his helm. 'Sometimes, Hylandris, you need to look at your feet, not the stars.'

'You might have given me instruction in the philoso-phies when I was younger, but in matters of foresight you must remember that I am now the tutor, not the pupil.'

'Forgive my impertinence, great master of the skein,' said Zarathuin with a mocking inclination of the head, 'but do the runes tell you, when we are cut off from the webway gate and our starship has crashed, how we are to get off this fates-forsaken moon with the prize?'

Hylandris said nothing, his mood soured by Zarathu-in's accusations. They descended without further words for some time, the wide stairwell lit by a ghostglow com-ing from the tip of the farseer's staff, the monotony of the many steps helping to centre his thoughts. The two seers passed level after level, each archway they passed sealed with flickering runes.

Eventually they stopped at one of the landings. Extend-ing his will, Hylandris opened the portal to reveal the interior of a gravity cage. Once they were inside the door closed and a shimmering field encapsulated the plat-form on which they stood. There was no sensation of movement, the walls of the descent tube being a uniform light grey, but the gravity conveyor was soon descend-ing at incredible speed.

'Of course,' said Zarathuin, 'it might not matter that we can't get back to the craftworld. If you can't find the solution to the vault key we might as well all die here anyway.'

The farseer turned his head to his companion. His ghosthelm concealed his grimace of distaste, but the rest of his posture conveyed his feelings well enough. Even so, he felt the need to put them into words.

'Have you nothing better to do than bait me with these jibes?'

Zarathuin returned his look, the farseer's reflection distorted in the yellow lenses of the warlock's helmet.

'Nothing until this pod reaches the vault level. Perhaps we could discuss why you think you can pit your skills of prescience against the greatest farseer our species has ever created? Why not simply ask Ulthran to help us avoid both fates? Oh, I remember. It's because you have already seen our victory. Tell me, during our philosophy lessons, did I ever tell you about circular arguments?'

'I despise you. I really do.'

8

There was silence in the small docking vestibule. The female shuddered as the words of the Phoenix Lord hit home. The rest of the crew looked on in stunned disbelief. Asurmen was used to such behaviour, an unavoidable effect of his nature. It was important not to allow distraction to impede his purpose.

'You are the pilot?' he asked.

'I am.' She seemed hesitant to confirm this fact. 'I am Neridiath.'

'I have need of your assistance,' the Phoenix Lord told her. He looked at the other members of the starship's crew. 'There is very little time to explain and we must get under way quickly. I need you to save questions for the moment. I must speak with Neridiath alone.'

The authority in his voice could not be gainsaid. Nodding numbly, eyeing the Phoenix Lord with amazement, the others left, leaving only the pilot with Asurmen.

Neridiath hugged her arms tightly about her body as

though she were cold. The Phoenix Lord realised it was his presence that disturbed her, his spirit like nothing she had encountered before. Asurmen knew from previous experience that he felt hollow to others. Not psychically dull like the humans and other mon-keigh, and not a complete void as Harlequin solitaires were sometimes described. Asurmen was simply *elsewhere*. His thoughts, his spirit permeated the armour, but she had no sense there was a living breathing person inside the suit.

'A wraith-construct,' he said suddenly, making Neridiath jump.

'Pardon?'

'The sensation you are feeling, I have been told it is similar to that experienced in the company of wraithguard, wraithlords and other spirit-walkers. I cannot confirm this as the sensation is very different for me, I expect. I find them... warm, perhaps.'

'I couldn't say, I've never been close to a wraith-construct.'

'You are fortunate, there are surprisingly few of our people that have not had to fight alongside the dead at one time or another. Increasingly so as the Rhana Dandra draws closer.'

'The end of the universe is close?' Neridiath looked terrified at the thought. She glanced back towards the door to the rest of the ship and Asurmen felt her thoughts flutter on the matrix, unconsciously seeking the infant he had detected when he had arrived. Her first thought was for her daughter but she suppressed it swiftly; her next words were strained. 'The last war against Chaos is about to begin?'

'My apologies, I view these matters in a different context. The Rhana Dandra is not fixed, but I have lived a long time and the last war is inevitably closer now than when the craftworlds first launched.'

'So, not in my lifetime?'

'No.'

'Manyia, my daughter?'

Asurmen looked down at the pilot, tilted his head slightly and shrugged.

'I can make no promise of that. I am a warrior, not a seer. Asuryan guides me, the Wisest of the Wise, but even he did not see all.'

'I thought Asuryan was dead, killed with the other gods? How can he guide you?'

'Through visions, which echo forwards through time from the moment he was killed. His final dream-patterns were impregnated onto a crystal and through that his gravest fears can be seen by me and the others of my kind.'

'This is too much to accept.' Neridiath held her head in her hands and started to pace, circling the Phoenix Lord in the small room. 'A warrior of legend turns up on my ship asking for help and starts talking about the Rhana Dandra, and being guided here by the last dreams of a dead god? What do you need me for? I missed that part. Perhaps you should start from the beginning.'

'I will, the very beginning if that is what you wish, but I do not have the time right now.' Asurmen held up his hand but withdrew it a moment before his fingers touched her, leaving her to continue pacing. 'I will tell you plainly what I need. A starship has crashed on a moon not far from here and the pilots have been rendered incapable of steering it back to orbit. I need you to launch that ship and destroy several enemy vessels.'

'I see. In one sense that is very clear, on the other...' Neridiath stopped walking and closed her eyes, visibly making an effort to remain calm. Asurmen wondered how he had come to such a position that the future of his people might wholly depend upon this one individual. He had to trust in Asuryan's wisdom, allow it to guide him without resistance. 'Rendered incapable? You mean killed?'

'Unfortunately not.' Honesty usually served fate better than manipulation. 'There was an accident, but they were not slain.'

The pilot shuddered visibly at the thought.

'I have to tell you that I will not fight. I am not a warrior.' Neridiath looked at him straight, her jaw set, hands forming fists. There was determination there, but also tension and fear. A lot of fear. 'It... It isn't in me. To kill. Not idly do the Phoenix Lords enter our lives. I would be a fool to refuse your request. You are a legend, all of the Asurya are. I could not say no to you any more than if Eldanesh himself resurrected and asked for my aid. I will help you rescue this starship, but I will not, cannot unleash that monster for you. If that is what you need, you must look elsewhere.'

'There are no others that can respond in time. The skein brought me to you, you to me,' Asurmen told her quietly. He could understand her reluctance to fight, but he was depending upon her to do so. The survival of the battleship was secondary to destroying the Obliterator Shards, but she did not need to know that. 'You must set course for Escatharinesh immediately. If we delay, all hope is lost.'

'Hope for whom? You? The ship's crew?' Neridiath

turned to the door but was stopped mid-step by the Phoenix Lord's next words.

'Our people. All of them. There is a war coming that must not escalate, otherwise none of us will survive to see the Rhana Dandra.'

'Oh.' Neridiath took a deep breath. 'Yes, you already said that. I thought, hoped, perhaps I had misheard.'

She looked at Asurmen, her strength wilting under the weight of this revelation. She looked momentarily lost and afraid, like the child for whom she cared so much. Sometimes Asurmen forgot that he and his kind had been in existence since before the Fall and had long grown accustomed to such notions as the Final Battle against Chaos and the end of the known universe. Neridiath was having trouble assimilating this information and words failed her.

He detected a gnawing terror growing inside her, confronted by the enormity of the universe in such abrupt fashion. He needed her to be sharp and focused, now and when the time came for her to act. Better to fix her thoughts on something more tangible.

'Your daughter needs you to do this. To safeguard her future.'

'I expect she does.'

Neridiath's breathing slowed and some measure of control returned at the thought of her child. Asurmen felt a moment of satisfaction. He always did when he saw his lessons, the teachings of the Path, being put into practice, even ten generations after he had first devised them.

'How am I supposed to deal with all of this? I am just a pilot, from a small craftworld. I do not think anyone from Anuiven has even seen a Phoenix Lord before, much less the legendary Asurmen himself.'

The pilot had a strong will, he could sense it, but it would be of no use if her mind was set against Asuryan's purpose. He had to make it seem less mythic, less overwhelming for her.

'Being an optimist helps,' said the Phoenix Lord. 'When you have survived the birth-hunger of a Chaos god everything else is a gift.'

'Comforting. Why don't you tell me about that while we head to the control pod? Please keep talking so that I don't have any time to think about what you've just told me, about the doom of our entire race resting on my shoulders.'

The door opened and Neridiath led Asurmen into the main part of the ship. Once inside the passageway she started to relax, comforted by her familiar surroundings. Her ease grew as they continued down the corridor. Asurmen felt the thoughts of the other crew filling the ship with a sense of belonging that dulled his otherworldly presence in the pilot's mind.

'My granted-name was Illiathin and I was born on the world of Eidafaeron,' he replied after giving the request some thought. 'I was an indolent youth and an even more self-absorbed adult.'

I

Along with a crowd of thousands, Illiathin stood on the vast stellar gallery and watched with wide eyes as a coronal ejection lashed out from the star. There were gasps and claps as the prominence of energised particles splashed across the gallery screens, enveloping everybody with a bright yellow glare. Almost as one, the crowd turned to follow the ejection's course out into the system, watching the massive lick of star-fire slowly dissipate into a gust of stellar wind.

At the last moment a flock of void-suited star-riders descended from their waiting ship. Some rode longboards, others had bodywings or dragchutes. Shimmering as the flare lapped against their personal shields, the star-riders caught the stellar draught and sped away, twisting, turning, performing tricks to outdo each other in skill and daring.

Illiathin gestured, summoning a lens field in the shield surrounding the viewing gallery. In the magnified display *he followed the progress of the star-riders, marvelling at their agility and bravery.*

'Ever been tempted?'

He turned as a stranger spoke to him. The eldar who approached was dressed in a figure-hugging black bodysuit beneath a voluminous puff of red-and-white sleeved cape. He looked past Illiathin at the figures dwindling in the view of the lens field.

'No, it looks far too much like effort,' Illiathin replied, realising the meaning of the question. 'Also, I hear it is dangerous. Shields can fail, a missed step or turn can get you flung towards a celestial body.'

'Fatalities are rare,' the stranger said. 'And if there is no risk, it lessens the reward. If you change your mind, beginners can take their first simulated rides at the Horn of Nemideth. My name is Kardollin, ask for me by name.'

'I will,' said Illiathin, with no intention of ever doing so.

Kardollin shrugged and memestrands in his cape stiffened, turning it into a broad set of wings. Illiathin detected the subtle pulse of a gravitic impeller as the other eldar took a step and floated into the air, catching the cross-gallery breeze to soar away with a backward glance and a smile.

The excitement of the coronal flare and the encounter with the star-rider was quite enough activity for Illiathin, so he sought a space at one of the many hostelries that lined the starward edge of the gallery. Choosing a venue at the very edge of the crowd, he was able to slip into a space recently vacated by another sunwatcher. The disc-like table grew a seating appendage at his approach, extruding itself a little further from the floor to compensate for Illiathin's long legs. Bathed in the field-dimmed light of the star, Illiathin sat and reviewed the holographic menu before mentally selecting a strong wine and a selection of confectionery to accompany it. Moments after the wish was made a floating tray brought his order to the table, its prehensile limb depositing the jug, glass and plate before him.

He enjoyed watching other people more than joining them. The gallery, one of his favourite haunts, was quiet compared to the many times he had been there before. Most of the stellar fanatics had left Eidafaeron to watch a supernova in Naethamesh a few hundred light years away. Illiathin had decided to forego the occasion, thinking it a little morbid to hold a festival in celebration of the death of a star.

He leaned back, the chair adjusting to his languid recline. Stretching out his legs, Illiathin indulged in his favourite pastime: doing nothing at all except watching others.

Among the throng he noticed a disturbance. People were parting like water before the bow of a sailing yacht. Into the gap strode a severe-looking figure, her hair bound tight with jewelled pins, her cheeks marked by vertical streaks of stylised red tears. Alone amongst the teeming eldar she wore a robe of white, the colour of death and mourning, but it was not this that caused the crowd to retreat from her approach. She was talking, not to herself, but to everyone nearby. Illiathin touched a hand to the lobe of his ear, activating the implants of his inner ear. Instantly he was able to focus on her words.

'...this shall not end in peace but in war with ourselves. Our great foe remains, within ourselves, when all others have been conquered. To what mischief will idle minds

turn? To what depravity will we stoop when our lives no longer have meaning? What sensation shall we crave when the exotic has become mundane?'

As the doomsayer turned towards Illiathin he realised too late that it was not her words that were driving folk away, as ridiculous as they were, but the glow of the projector lenses fitted into her eyes. The moment he met her stare the psychoprojectors reached into his mind, conjuring up a scene from his own subconscious.

He saw himself being burned alive by the stellar flare, each layer of his body stripped away an atom at a time. He watched in horror as skin, then fat, then muscle was flensed away, all that he was consumed by the fiery passion of the star. And then came the realisation that it was not the star that devoured him, but his own passions and desires, and that they were eating away inside him, hollowing out his spirit. Into this emptiness poured a filthy black fog, polluting his body, corrupting everything that he was.

Breaking away from her gaze with an effort of will, Illiathin rose to his feet with an angry shout.

'You're insane!' he yelled. 'Fates-forsaken doom-monger, ply your misery elsewhere!'

The crowd was turning from agitated to hostile, the calls of derision becoming louder, a few threats thrown in with the denouncements.

'Heed our words and know that our destroyer stalks us,' the doomsayer shrieked, ducking as something was thrown at her. She had time to hurl one last warning before turning and running, pursued by a hail of insults and a few improvised missiles. 'The exodus is coming. Only those that join us will be saved!'

Her departure was followed by a hubbub of whispered curses and murmured displeasure. Illiathin turned to the table next to his, where a young couple were holding hands, their faces pensive as they watched the doomsayer disappear into the throng. He saw in their expressions fear and hesitant belief. Most of the doomsayers were young and rebellious, conflating frustration at a lack of personal philosophy with an inherent weakness in wider society.

'Don't pay her any heed,' Illiathin told the couple. 'You'll find something of meaning in your lives. We all do eventually.'

They left with polite, unconvinced smiles and Illiathin watched them go. He sat down and took a mouthful of wine. Illiathin savoured the tastes for some time, eyes closed. He swallowed and lifted the goblet in mock salute to the departed doomsayer, the dire vision she had hurled into his thoughts already fading.

'Life's too long to spend it being miserable.'

9

'It's too dangerous,' announced Laurennin. 'Reaching the planet is going to be impossible.'

'You cannot be serious,' said Taerathu. 'Asurmen said that billions of our people will die if we do not rescue that starship.'

'He could be wrong,' said Laurennin. He darted a look at the immobile figure standing in the corner of the room. He squirmed as he uttered the words, seeming to hate himself for voicing them but forced by his cowardice to do so. 'Or exaggerating, or both. How can one starship be that important?'

'He is the Hand of Asuryan,' Neridiath said, her sharp voice cutting across the debate for the first time since the crew had gathered to discuss their new arrival.

The merchant and Neridiath's crew sat and stood around the largest of the *Joyous Venture*'s three communal chambers. Fael played with Manyia while Neridiath did her best to stop the debate becoming an outright argument. They had arrived at their destination, sliding from the webway into the outer system so that Kaydaryal's sensors could locate the enemy ships. There seemed little chance of bypassing them to reach the crashed battleship and several of the crew had baulked at the danger, despite being called upon to do so by a bona fide legend.

The Phoenix Lord stood to one side, saying nothing. His presence lent an air of gravitas to the discussion, as though fate itself hinged on every word. It was not altogether a welcome sensation and Neridiath felt nervous under his scrutiny.

'Do you really think you can live with yourself if we just turn tail and run?' asked Fael. 'You want to give up just because there might be some risk?'

'Some risk?' Tharturin was in Laurennin's camp and stood behind the merchant's chair, one hand on his shoulder. 'We cannot fight warships, each of which is more than capable of destroying us, and we have to get past them twice. That's assuming that we can find the battleship and that it can actually take off when we get there.'

'I can't imagine these ships can outrun us,' said Taerathu. 'For a start they would need to build up momentum from orbit – we could be halfway back to the webway before they've even broken out of the gravity thrall.'

'What about missiles and torpedoes? Can we outrun them?' said Laurennin.

'You are all missing the point,' Asurmen said suddenly. The room fell silent as they all waited on his next words. 'The battleship is capable of defending itself and destroying the enemy vessels. Your reluctance is unhelpful, your concern a needless obstacle. In fact, your compliance is unnecessary. I have not asked for your aid, only the pilot's. It is her decision. Neridiath, we waste precious time with this indulgence.'

'We have been called and must answer, said Neridiath, stirred by Asurmen's prompting. It was hard to argue with a legend. 'The world was once ours, we need not risk open void. The webway extends through the system, to the ground itself if need be. We will use the tendril to get into orbit and then emerge to scan the surface and find this battleship. Kaydaryal, join me in the control pod.'

She ignored the protests that followed her out of the room, the matrix pulsing with conflicting emotions of excitement and concern. Despite their misgivings, the crew complied and took up their positions while Neridiath assumed the piloting duties and Kaydaryal interfaced with the scanners.

The pilot pulsed a message out into the ship's matrix, seeking Asurmen. A heartbeat later she felt the telltale chill of his presence, albeit psychically rather than physically.

'You said that humans had attacked the ship we are seeking,' Neridiath remarked. 'Those we detected were not human in origin.'

Of a sort, the Phoenix Lord replied. *The humans are under the sway of a dark mistress sworn to the Powers of Chaos. It seems that she desires that which lies beneath the surface of the world, an ancient weapon from before the Fall. It is the promise of this prize that has bought her an army. The humans have a name for them: the Vanguard. They are like a plague in certain parts of the human-held galaxy, following no greater cause than to fight on behalf of the Dark Gods with whichever champion rises amongst them. They are cosmic flotsam. The craftworld of Thiestha was nearly destroyed by them, and earned them the name the Flesh-thieves. They have brought with them fragments of an ancient weapon, a device of Chaos that should have been destroyed. Chance, or fate, brings them to this world at the same time as the expedition from Anuiven.*

'You never mentioned the starship is from our craftworld!'

Is it important? My desire is to benefit all of our people. The politics of the craftworlds is not my concern. The rescue of the ship is a catalyst, not an end – the consequences of what happens here reach far beyond the demesne of Anuiven.

'You are right, this is more important than the affairs of a single craftworld. It doesn't change the fact that the enemy ships are clearly something more than I was expecting. There is no way we'll be able to get a starship past them.'

The plan is sound. Follow the webway as far as you can and we will exit close to the moon. We will move into material space when the satellite's position shields us from detection.

Faced with such conviction, she was left in no doubt about their course of action. Neridiath pushed away the psychic link and concentrated on guiding the *Joyous Venture* along the narrowing webway tunnel that curved towards the system's major planets.

It took most of the rest of the cycle to traverse the star system to their destination and Neridiath was tired. An abrupt message from Kaydaryal brought her back to her full senses.

'A taint on the webway,' the navigator hissed beside her. Kaydaryal's thoughts projected across the ship. 'Fael, get to your post.'

Neridiath quickly took stock of the situation. Kaydaryal's assessment was correct, there was some kind of warp-leak infecting the terminus of the webway ahead. She slowed the *Joyous Venture*, unsure what to do.

We have to turn back, said Laurennin. *That is Chaos-taint! Would you doom us all for vanity?*

'We only need to pass through for a moment,' said Neridiath. 'If we leave the webway now, we'll be detected before we reach the moon.'

It is the Chaos vessels. Asurmen's thoughts were calm and reassuring. *They exist partially within the warp and their presence buckles the wards that guard the webway.*

Neridiath accelerated again, allowing the *Joyous Venture* to reach top speed. She tapped into Kaydaryal's mind to look ahead at the encroaching Chaos corruption around the exit gate. Normally she would not leave the webway at full speed, there was too much danger of colliding with a celestial object in real space. The tendrils of dark energy seeping through the fabric of the webway sent a chill through her, leaving no option but to power through and hope for the best.

She placed her faith in Asurmen, and the belief that he would not have brought them here simply to die, his mission unfulfilled. Where Asurmen walked, victory followed. That was the legend.

The thickening roots of the Chaos incursion suddenly sprouted thorny vines that speared along the webway towards the approaching ship. Neridiath reacted, detaching the matrix from the psychic wall to drift through the webway gate, but she was too late. A fragment of the Chaos energy lodged in the matrix like a thorn from a bush pricking skin.

'Get it out!' she snapped, her thoughts moving to Fael. Her companion initiated the psychic defences, shutting down every system across the ship except life support. Silvery energy flowed from the matrix core, cleansing, burning the infiltrating motes of corrupting power. The taint was contained but the threat was not. The Chaos-thorn grew a lashing psychic tail, latching onto the black tendrils of its parent taint, slowing the *Joyous Venture*.

Neridiath could not access the engines without feeding more psychic energy to the shrivelling Chaos-thorn and the starship slowed to an agonising stop as more tendrils enveloped it, the webway gate fully dilated just a short distance ahead.

'Push through!' snarled Fael. 'Push through! It can't hurt us once we're in r–'

He did not finish what he was saying. Something noxious hurled itself through the matrix and into his mind, splaying out through his thoughts like a virulent infection. Neridiath cut off contact with Fael out of instinct and physically recoiled, the piloting harness unfolding to deposit her on the deck of the pod. Fael was dead in the embrace of his gunner's couch, eyes black pools, his skin dry like dead leaves.

The walls were fading, the warp energy leaking through to pool like water on the floor. Something was forming from the sludge, a grotesque humanoid figure made of blackness and blood.

Run!

Asurmen's impulse flared through Neridiath. She turned and grabbed Kaydaryal, who was stumbling from her cradle-point. The two of them fled the control pod as more daemons manifested behind them.

The two of them headed down to the main deck, almost falling over each other as they descended the steep stairway. Kaydaryal headed aft, seeking the others, but Neridiath turned back towards the prow, to her chambers. The floors and ceiling of the passageways were contorting, shapes moving beneath the surface like trapped air bubbles. Here and there the bubbles cracked open like obscene eggs, grasping hands and tentacles forming from the pus and bile within.

Neridiath felt like screaming, but she held the terror at bay with a single thought: Manyia.

The door to her personal chambers cycled open at her approach and Neridiath dashed inside. Her daughter was where she had been left, in her cot. The floor beneath was like a dark pool and the bed was sinking, the legs disappearing into inky shadow. Manyia was waking, disturbed by the deadening of the matrix.

Her fear lending speed to her thoughts and deeds, Neridiath waded into the blackness that had consumed the floor of the room. She snatched Manyia from the cot and turned back, but it was like walking through tar. Eyes materialised in the surface of the warp-pool and claws and maws opened, flexing and gurgling.

Reaching the doorway, Neridiath dragged herself free, only to find the route aft blocked. Daemon apparitions thronged the corridor, at least a dozen of them. Though the matrix was shut down, Neridiath caught the faint wash of death and terror from the other crew across the *Joyous Venture*. The ship was being overrun.

Something hot touched the back of her neck and she glanced over her shoulder to see a monstrous fiend heaving itself out of the mire that had been her rooms. Slug-like, but with spindly arms and rows of jointed legs, the daemon-thing formed out of the oozing Chaos filth.

They were trapped. A panicked thought caused the chamber door to slide shut, but Neridiath knew it was only a physical barrier, no defence against the immaterial invaders. Manyia was whimpering and wide-eyed with fear. They were both going to die here.

No sooner had the thought come to Neridiath than a white fire blazed along the corridor.

Asurmen was there, sword in his hand, his shuriken vambraces sending slashing salvoes through the daemons. He looked different here, where the warp overlap was tearing apart what was real and what was dream. To Neridiath it appeared a white-clad knight cut and thrust through the mass of daemons, the blade in his hands a burning pale flame that fed on the energy of the daemons it touched.

She saw his face, or the imagining of his face. He was handsome, his jaw set in determination, eyes piercing blue points of light. The image faded, leaving the blue armoured figure she had known since an early age.

The corridor was empty, the daemons banished for the moment. Where Asurmen passed, the taint recoiled from his presence, like a plant touched by too much sun, withering and flaking.

'We have to run,' said Asurmen, taking her wrist in his hand. She flinched at the touch but found it oddly warm and comforting.

'Can you kill them?' she asked.

'The ship is trapped. It is lost. We must leave in my vessel.'

'What about the others?' Neridiath pulled her hand free as Asurmen set off down the corridor, blade glowing in his other hand.

'I need you to live,' the Phoenix Lord replied. 'No other. We have to escape and save the battleship.'

Neridiath was frozen to the spot, horrified by the thought of abandoning her companions. She was broken from the trance as a wet exhalation flowed through the opening door behind her. With a shriek she started to run. Asurmen forged ahead of her with half a dozen long strides.

They headed down, towards the berth where Asurmen's ship was latched onto the *Joyous Venture*. Daemons assailed them, some shapeless, clawed and fanged monstrosities, others humanoid with cyclopean faces and rusted blades. Asurmen never broke pace, cutting down every intruder that crossed his path. Neridiath felt herself dragged along in his wake, drawn through the nightmarishly contorting ship by the force of his will and the strength of his sword arm.

A cluster of daemons was crowded around the boarding portal, kept at bay by a shining light from beyond the connecting chamber. The barrier wavered as the daemons lashed their anger upon it, bright cobalt coruscations thrown up by every blow.

Asurmen fell upon the daemons with his blade, each stroke felling an attacker, every movement precise and deadly.

The Phoenix Lord grabbed Neridiath's arm and almost

tossed her through the portal. As she passed the shield around his ship she had a sensation of falling. She almost tripped as she found the deck beneath her feet after a moment. Asurmen stepped backwards through the psychic barrier, firing shurikens at some unseen foe further along the passageway.

Come aboard.

The ship's words entered Neridiath's thoughts, a command rather than an invitation. She plunged through the docking link and onto the Phoenix Lord's vessel. Asurmen followed on her heel, his blade hissing with vibrant life. The moment they were both aboard the portal sliced closed and Neridiath felt a lurch as the ship detached itself from the *Joyous Venture*.

'Hurry, we cannot withstand the incursion much longer,' said Asurmen. It took a moment for Neridiath to realise he was speaking to the ship. 'We must break free of the webway.'

II

Gently placing his fingers on the veined surface of the contact pad, Illiathin allowed his mind to flow into the soaring dream-tree. The tree was as white as snow, with deeply ridged bark. But in the depths of those folds glittered traces of crystallised sap. In places the crystals grew like fungus, fronds and pods that stood out from the pale surface. A branch contorted around his body, supporting him as he relaxed, letting his mind go further, drifting into the heartwood of the dream-tree.

Laughter drew him on, up through the tree and into the higher boughs. From here he could feel the wind swaying his branches, and the moisture on his leaves. The mists swirled as limbs spread out in the dawning sun, and he felt the surge of strength as heat touched upon the leaves.

There were others with him, each sharing in the dream-tree's awakening. Some, like Illiathin, were alive still, using the contact pads to commune with the psychic tree. Many were dead, in body at least. Their remains had been buried beneath the island-spanning root system of the dream-tree, their spirits taken up into it as a normal tree would siphon water.

There were hundreds in this dream-tree alone, seeking a form of immortality. Illiathin could feel them, pulses of energy alongside his, not quite aware or conscious, as much memory as thought. But they lived on in essence, granted an eternity to continue to experience the universe, albeit it second-hand.

Illiathin shared no such desire himself. Life was long enough, even longer if he wanted to regrow or join the growing numbers of the reborn. The natural span of his people, already measured in hundreds of stellar orbits, had been extended tenfold, a hundredfold even, by the technologies they had invented over the aeons. The gift of Vaul, the knowledge of artifice, had made them masters of the stars and their own bodies.

Illiathin was not like those that embraced longevity for its own sake. There were some eldar that sought to out-live even the stars, being rebirthed again and again and again down the ages. Illiathin had no time for a universe without stars. What a cold, empty place that would be. The Immortal Intellects, as they were sometimes known, argued that thought and will existed in isolation to the physical. They alone would know how the universe would end, and were willing to endure eternity to see it.

Not for Illiathin such a tedious existence. He was no sensationalist, like the star-riders or the war-thieves and void-chasers, but one life was hard enough to fill with meaningful interaction. The thrill of danger held no allure for him, but he had lived long enough that the simple pleasures he knew were starting to bore him.

On the other end of the scale, he wondered how the lesser races coped, with illness ravaging them, and the predations of age making their bodies infirm long before it took its last toll. They seemed so desperate to explore, to battle, to breed. Their time was so short, their lives so pointlessly brief.

There were some amongst the eldar that envied the lower creatures this vigorous existence, extolling the virtues of toil and endeavour. The worst were the doomsayers. Joyless pessimists, their forecasts of a collapse in society and civilisation would be ludicrous if there were not so many of them. They had become like a plague in recent times, and now the disillusioned youths had some politically powerful sympathisers.

Worlds were being seeded in their cause, on the far fringe of civilisation, close to the barbarian species. Such a waste of resources, but if the doomsayers wanted to run away to the darkest corners of the galaxy to live out their time in miserable labour and crude hardship, that was their prerogative. They were just as entitled to their own particular mania as the bodyshifters, warpwalkers, turnskins and the other vagabonds and fanatics.

The dawnlight was almost full, the energy of the dream-tree pulsing strongly from tip of root to end of branch. Dead spirits were on the move, flashing past and through Illiathin, glorying in another spring after the long turn of winter.

Illiathin had been told that a dream-tree wakening was one of the experiences of a lifetime, but he was underwhelmed. He had mind-shifted into many different guises and bodies, and the semi-mobile appendages of a tree seemed very constricting. It certainly did not compare to *riding the mind of a golden falcon over the mountains of Tybraenesh, and it paled next to hunting as a dagger-fin in the lava flows of Lashartarekh.*

The touch of the dead was cold and clammy, spoiling what could have been a worthwhile experience. Instead of living with the moment of growth and resurgence that the dream-tree felt, he recoiled from the sensation, discon-certed by the morbid presence of the deceased.

It is the juxtaposition that gives the experience mean-ing. Life and death entwined, inseparable.

A surge of happiness buoyed up Illiathin as he recog-nised the thoughts of the other living eldar.

Tethesis! *Using the dream-tree as an intermediary, he opened up his mind, inviting his brother to share the sen-sation. To Illiathin's disappointment, Tethesis withdrew, refusing the offer.*

I was told I would find you here, Illith. I have to talk to you. It is very important. I am on a contact pad near to you – come back to your body.

Before Illiathin could refuse or agree, Tethesis's spirit was gone, shrinking back to his physical shell. Illiathin drank in one last draught of the dream-tree's life, feeling the immensity of its existence, pushing aside the dead chill in its heart to enjoy the light falling on a billion quiver-ing leaves.

Annoyed at his brother's interruption – an encounter that could have been so much more pleasurable – Illiathin slid down the heartwood and back into his body. It took a moment for his consciousness to establish itself again. When he was fully integrated with his mortal form, the dream-tree relinquished its embrace and Illiathin opened his eyes. He looked first to the right, but saw nobody he recognised amongst the throng standing under the deep shadow of the dream-tree's boughs.

To the left were more strangers.

Confused, Illiathin searched the dream-arborealists more closely, looking at their faces. One of them was coming towards him and he flinched at the sight – a doomsayer in stark white, the red-streak tears and black-ened hair standing out amongst the bright colours of the other spring celebrants.

Then he recognised his younger brother's features beneath the scarlet, unrecognised at first because of the unfamiliar scowl and clenched jaw.

'Oh, Tethesis,' whispered Illiathin. 'Who have you been listening to?'

10

The camp of the Flesh-thieves was easy to find, a swathe of broken trees that spread like a stain through the forest that covered the foothills. In the pre-dawn gloom the glow of crude oil-burning stoves and lanterns lit the encampment with a sickly yellow glare, casting shadows from the bulk of dormant armoured vehicles and high-sided tents.

Their name was not just poetic. Flapping tatters of skin marked with perverse daubing and profane sigils served as standards for the various groups and warbands that made up the army. Braziers hissed and sputtered with fat scraped from the corpses of their victims. The vellum-like tents and pavilions were stitched together by braids of human and eldar hair, the swirls of dead mouths and ears and eyeholes sewn up with gizzard-string.

The whole clearing would have reeked of the macabre ornamentation and Nymuyrisan was glad he could smell nothing within the confines of the wraithknight. Even so, the sight turned his stomach.

The artillery guns that had been shelling the site of the *Patient Lightning*'s landing for the past six planetary rotations were lined up five deep in rows along the edge of the huge clearing. Their crews slept in bivouacs beside the great guns, alongside sandbagged magazines filled with shells.

The Flesh-thieves themselves were oddly devoid of trophies. They wore an assortment of menial clothes, uniforms from different human organisations, worlds and regiments. They were little more than stray animals bound into a pack by the charisma and power of the Dark Lady.

Nymuyrisan led the attack, the towering wraithknight stepping as easily between the trees as if the elegant giant body were his own. He could feel the spirit of Jarithuran flowing through him even as his own spirit flowed through the spirit stones powering the immense construct. It helped to have his brother close on occasions like this, although the pain of his twin's death lingered still on the edge of his mind. Jarithuran responded to this line of thought, surfacing from his dormant state to offer wordless reassurance and encouragement.

Skimming Falcon grav-tanks followed behind the wraithbone giant, moving swiftly and silently into position, spreading out around the perimeter of the camp. They remained out of sight of the sentries for the time being, masked from the humans' simple scanners by the trees and countermeasures far more advanced than the sensors of their foes. In their wake came a handful of Wave Serpent transports, their elongated troop compartments filled with Aspect Warriors.

The servants of Khaine stayed in reserve, to be deployed

only if needed. This was to be a swift attack, wreaking destruction on the artillery that had beset the battleship, and then withdrawing. If the eldar had to commit infantry to the attack, their withdrawal would be far more prolonged and dangerous.

'Surprise, speed and surety,' Nymuyrisan announced across the etheric communication network, repeating the words Farseer Hylandris had impressed upon him before the departure. 'Pick your targets with precision and watch for each other. We will teach the mon-keigh that they rouse our wrath with their impudent attacks. They will rue the coming of the dawn.'

With a final check that his fellow eldar were in place, Nymuyrisan let the power of the wraithknight's core flow into the long limbs, breaking into a run. He was one with the semi-living machine, its sensors filtering the external data into his thoughts, creating a shifting, ethereal view of his environment. Even before visual sensors could detect the enemy, heat and motion scanners were pinpointing possible targets. Red silhouettes highlighted their positions, while pale-blue blurs showed him where the eldar forces were approaching.

Nymuyrisan trusted his brother to keep the wraithknight moving and assumed control of the twin starcannons mounted on the war machine's shoulders. Hails of plasma spat from the weapons, flickering blue blasts that ignited one of the ammunition stores. The detonation lit up the camp with bright fire, rousing the Chaos followers more surely than any shout or alarm.

The strobing red rays of pulse lasers from the Falcons followed Nymuyrisan into the clearing, picking out the self-propelled guns and dismounted cannons. The wraithknight pressed on, the first bursts of return fire glancing ineffectually from its curved exoskeletal plates. Lifting a hoof-like foot, Jarithuran stamped down on a small personnel transport, crushing its engine block and bending the axles. A spring in its step, the wraithknight powered on, starcannons firing again at a communications pylon close to the centre of the encampment.

A sense of alarm from Jarithuran warned Nymuyrisan of a human tank coming to life to their right. A heat plume from its engines shone scarlet amongst the cluster of sensor returns. Jarithuran turned as Nymuyrisan aimed the starcannons. The storm of plasma splashed across the thick frontal armour of the tank, scorching metal but not penetrating. The turret rotated laboriously towards them, its muzzle lit by the flicker of a tracking laser.

Conjoined even after death, the twins reacted as one. Jarithuran pushed the wraithknight to the left, back past the swinging gun barrel, while Nymuyrisan lifted up the gleaming blade in the wraithknight's right hand. The tank fired, its shot a blur past the wraithknight's shoulder.

Nymuyrisan could feel the men inside the tank labouring quickly to load another shell. He could sense their panic and felt a sharp spike in the fear as dread-hastened fingers dropped the shell before it could be placed into the breach. The driver slammed the tank into reverse and backed away with tracks spewing churned mud.

The wraithknight was far faster, Jarithuran closing the distance in five long strides. A secondary weapon, some kind of rapid bullet-firer, growled into life, but Nymuyrisan had the left arm raised protectively in front of them, its scattershield generator glowing with multicoloured light. The spray of bullets slammed into the projected field. Converted into energy, they exploded into a rainbow bright enough to momentarily blind anyone looking at it.

The tank crew's desperation was palpable as the wraithknight reached its target. One of them tried to scramble out of the turret hatch, only to be snatched up in the wraithknight's left hand. Crushing the Chaos worshipper to a pulp, Nymuyrisan tossed the bloody remnants away and readied the ghostglaive. He remembered how wrong it had felt at first, using the spirit energy of his dead brother to power the glowing blade, but now he barely gave the matter a second thought.

The first cut sheared through the barrel of the tank's cannon. The second plunged down through the top of the turret, slicing into the ammunition store near the base of the armoured vehicle.

The explosion wrapped the wraithknight in a storm of flaming debris, scoring burned welts across the surface of its body and slender limbs. Nymuyrisan felt a pulse of admonition from his twin and offered up thoughts of apology in reply.

Turning, they came across another tank, unmanned. At Jarithuran's urging, the wraithknight crouched down and grabbed hold of a track mounting. Lifting up the tank, they tore the track and running wheels free before carving the engine in half with the ghostglaive. A second and then a third suffered a similar fate before Nymuyrisan felt the tingle of the communications matrix dragging him back out of the battle-trance.

In that moment he sensed that two-thirds of the artillery had already been destroyed. The Flesh-thieves were swarming like ants from a disrupted nest, dragging out heavy weapons, dashing for their vehicles heedless of the storm of laser fire and shurikens that cut down their comrades. Nymuyrisan could see little in their armoury that could harm the wraithknight, but the Falcon crews were concerned about the swiftness and size of the humans' retaliation.

'Exit and I shall guard the withdrawal,' Nymuyrisan told them, bringing up the scattershield.

Walking backwards through the blazing ruins of the tanks, crushing underfoot any human foolish enough to come too close, the wraithknight backed away from the camp, unleashing bursts from its starcannons. Tank shells screamed from the scattershield in blazes of light, the flares of blinding luminescence further hampering the humans' woeful targeting. Behind the wraith-construct, the eldar tanks and transports slipped away into the forest, their mission complete.

With a last storm of plasma scything through the gathering platoons of soldiers, Nymuyrisan and Jarithuran guided the wraithknight back into the trees, enemy fire setting alight the foliage around them. Nymuyrisan raised the ghostglaive in a mocking salute, the flames of the burning camp reflected along the blade. They turned and broke into a run, soon hidden by tall trees, leaving behind a glow from the burning camp brighter than the radiance of the approaching dawn.

III

'It's ugly.'

Silhouetted against the glow of the dormant webgate pylons the starship was an elongated disc. The line of its upper surface was broken by short towers and hemispherical domes. The underside had an ungainly bulge towards the stern where the gravity engines were housed. Illiathin knew that there could be a form of imperfect beauty in asymmetry, the imbalance of form creating something powerful and dynamic. The ship of the Exodites possessed none of those aspects.

'It is functional,' replied Tethesis. He was dressed in his white robe, feet bare on the marbled red and grey of the orbital dock's boarding bridge.

'Style does not have to impede function. The habitat towers could be taller, for a start. That would offset the bulk of the gravity motors underneath. And the domes are so small. They look like warts almost.'

'When we arrive at Thurassimenesh, the ship will be

the foundation of our new city. We will not have gravitic impellers to reach cloud-touching towers, we will ascend by steps. The domes can be detached and used to form satellite settlements. We will be using physical labour to move them. Domesticated animals and the like. Any larger and they will be impossible to carry.'

Illiathin looked around and saw clusters of other eldar moving up the three boarding bridges to the starship. Many were dressed in the white robes associated with the Exodites, as the doomsayers styled themselves, but there were several dozen at least in regular garb.

'The newly inspired,' explained Tethesis as he followed his brother's gaze.

'Inspired? Deluded more like.' Illiathin looked back towards the shuttle-yacht that had brought him to the outer-system dock.

'Do you not wish to leave?'

'Leave?' Illiathin laughed. 'With you? I assume that is why you asked me to come here.'

'I wished to have one last opportunity to impress upon you the folly of doing nothing. Please, Illith, come with us. With me. You do not have to accept the truth of the Exodus, but what harm could it do? I fear for you, Illith. For everyone.'

'I have better things to do with my life than spend it cutting down trees and shovelling reptile dung.'

'Better things, or easier things?' Tethesis bared his teeth in annoyance. 'What meaning do our lives have? We do not strive any more. Spirit-drones and psychomatons explore and conquer in our name and we reap the rewards of an empire of ten thousand stars. To what do we aspire? What point is there in living this way?'

'To honour those that could not enjoy such times,' Illi-athin snapped back. 'Generations that lived and died on starships to seed the world we inhabit. Forefathers that travelled the cold gulf between stars to harness the web-way gates that stretch from one end of civilisation to the other. Millions that died fighting wars against countless mon-keigh species, dying to create peace for those that came after. We should remember them, not emulate them.'

'How can you understand anything of what they did if you have not even the slightest common experience? You have never set foot outside this star system, what do you know of forging an empire in the stars?'

'I know that I have no care for it! Wear your heavy robes and walk barefoot upon the ground, but it does not mean you are any closer to the heirs of Eldanesh than I. You are as conceited as any other if you think you have found the key to happiness.'

'Happiness? It is not happiness we seek, it is grief. The grief of life being lived, the cessation of which has been earned, not inherited. We go to build paradise, brother.'

'Then go, and spare me your lectures.'

Sadness fell across Tethesis's features. He looked over his shoulder at the Exodite ship. Dozens of lights were springing up through circular windows along the rim of the disc. Returning his gaze to Illiathin, he sighed.

'I cannot leave without you, Illith.'

'You must have known that I would not come. Why drag me all the way to the edge of the system to hear it?'

'Look, look at the stars, brother.'

Illiathin turned away from the starship and the webway portal, his back to the system's star so that he looked out from the asteroid-girdling dock into the depths of outer space. He knew he was looking towards the rim of the galaxy, where the stars were thinly spread, but still hundreds of them glittered like diamonds on black cloth. The thin enclosed atmosphere of the orbital station did little to distort the incoming light, leaving each star stark and sharp in the inky darkness.

'Do they not call to you, brother?' asked Tethesis. 'A new world, a new beginning?'

'An old argument,' replied Illiathin, letting his annoyance show as he turned back to his brother. 'Do not think that you can coerce me into joining you. I am not your guardian, I make no claim over what you do. If you wish to go, then go, follow your convictions, but do not use them as a lever to change my purpose.'

'I will remain because I do consider myself your guardian. I have realised that I cannot leave you. It would be selfish beyond regard to abandon you.'

'I do not need your protection, or your pity. Stay if you want to, that is your decision. I want nothing more to do with you. Leave me be.'

Illiathin turned away and strode back up the docking bridge, back towards the yacht. He was not sure which vexed him most – that his brother had dared to invite him on this ridiculous expedition, or the fact that for a heartbeat, as he had stared out into the stars, he had almost said yes.

11

There was always a moment, a tiny fraction of an instant, between the real and the unreal, between life and death, each time Neridiath transitioned from the webway into the mortal realm or the reverse. Her spirit stone, the crystal soul-jewel that would capture her essence at the moment of death, became a tiny sun for that moment, bright and hot on her chest.

It did not matter whether she was in the piloting cradle, experiencing the transition as part of the ship, or elsewhere just as a passenger. The sensation never changed, a coldness in the deepest part of her spirit, the leeching of the void. Everything seemed dim and lifeless for several moments after, as though vitality had been drained from the universe.

Asurmen's ship felt the change as much as any living eldar, bursting free from the webway like a seed expelled from a pod, its infrastructure alive with psychic energy. The warm embrace of the webway gave way to the vast emptiness of the real universe, a dizzying experience even for a seasoned pilot like Neridiath. And just as it took her a while to recover her wits and senses, so, too, did the starship need some time to reel back its psychic engines and activate the gravity drive. The solar sails unfurled, a golden reflective mesh of tiny hexagons that converted the particle energy of the stellar wind into power for the gravity impeller. Physical detectors took over from psychic senses.

Neridiath felt an invitation from the ship and slipped part of her consciousness into the newly awakened sensor arrays. Everything else was blocked off, access to the wider matrix denied. The most immediate phenomenon was the closing webway rift, torn open by the ship itself, something very difficult to accomplish.

Blocking out the waves of unnatural energy that streamed from the sealing portal Asurmen linked his mind to hers, the mental equivalent of taking her hand, and directed her attention to three anomalous, jagged shards in orbit over the third world, close by. They were star vessels, but like nothing Neridiath had seen or heard of before, like gigantic slivers of black ice retro-fitted with plasma engines, the striated hulls pocked with dozens of weapons turrets.

'What are they?' asked Neridiath.

Shards. Pieces of something far more deadly, replied Asurmen. *They are dangerous, but not so dangerous as they will become if we do not destroy them here. I detect no scanning from them, they appeared focused on the planet's surface.*

'Is it just me or do they feel... alive?' There was something about the ships that was, while not organic as such, certainly not entirely inert. A consciousness.

There is an awareness of sorts, but no more than in our vessels. There are crew aboard. The scanning streams focused on the nearest vessel. Hundreds of tiny pinpricks of red illuminated the outline of the enemy ship, labouring at gun decks that had been fastened to the sides of the central structure, and in the bowels of the Shard itself. Neridiath could see a dense cluster of creatures near the jagged prow and concluded that it had to be the control bridge.

The view dimmed and Neridiath felt herself eased out of the ship's system.

'You have been placed under my protection, Neridiath and Manyia,' the ship said in a clipped tone. Its voice was soft but the words abrupt, as though their presence were an inconvenience. 'I am *Stormlance*, steed of Asurmen. I am not large but I must guide you to your quarters. I have a very powerful matrix drive and several weapons systems that are dangerous. You must restrict your movements to the chambers I am about to show you.'

The lighting changed, the red brightening to yellow except for a faint scarlet line leading down the passageway to the left, towards the stern of *Stormlance*. Asurmen moved towards the prow but continued to monitor his visitors through the portion of his spirit that resided in the starship.

'Your quarters are this way,' *Stormlance* told them while they followed the wavering line towards their rooms. Manyia looked around, mouth gaping in amusement.

Nice.

'Not really,' said Neridiath, suspicious of the ship's nature.

'I have been built to destroy but I can also defend,' said

Stormlance, picking up on her doubts. 'I am a warship, a weapon. I am blameless for the purpose to which I am put, but rest assured that Asurmen, my master, wields me for a good cause.'

'What good can come of slaying?' Neridiath countered. 'Death is an end, not a beginning. To bring death is to end promise, to destroy potential.'

'Not always. To kill one while protecting another ensures a different promise, protects a different potential. Your simplistic morality is a luxury we cannot afford. It is an affectation – you cannot surely be this stupid.'

Neridiath bit back a retort as the ship brought them to a door that led to a narrow cabin. Inside, the floor moulded into two couches and a table, and opposite, another door led into a second chamber where there was a berth to either side, shelves and drawers fitted into the wall for the meagre possessions Neridiath had on her during their flight from their former ship.

'It occurs to me that if you can fly this ship, you could pilot the battleship,' she said aloud, addressing the Phoenix Lord. 'Why do you need me?'

'He cannot pilot the battleship,' replied *Stormlance*. 'His spirit is bound to his armour. He cannot release it to invest a ship's systems as you do.'

'Then how does he pilot you?'

There was a welling of humour, like a laugh without sound, edged with cruel humour. 'I do not have a pilot. I fly myself. I am Asurmen's steed, a part of the Phoenix Lord but separate. This shell is but the latest of many.'

'You are part of him?' Neridiath recoiled as though the walls were suddenly slick with filth. 'Which part?'

'The part he must give up to remain himself.' A savage

joy accompanied these words. There was a pause, no more than a few heartbeats, and the ship spoke again. 'We are under way.'

'Are we going to be in danger?'

'Yes,' said the ship. Its structure pulsed with the sensation of expectation, almost anticipation. 'Yes, there will be danger.'

12

Through the internal systems of *Stormlance*, Asurmen studied the pilot while they approached the moon on which the battleship had crashed, using the celestial body as a mask against the Shards' detectors.

He harboured doubts about her, particularly Neridiath's nature. She seemed self-obsessed, or at least self-involved. It was reasonable for her to protect her daughter, but it was not just caution that drove the pilot, there was something else behind her stubbornness, a suppressed fear that could explode at any time. Weighed against that was necessity. She was the only individual anywhere close to getting to the beset battleship in time. Asurmen had failed to prevent the war beginning; he was determined that it would not spiral out of control. Neridiath would pilot the battleship, even if Asurmen had to die again to make it happen.

She was playing with her daughter, Manyia. The infant's laughter filled the small warship as she moved hesitantly from one foot to the other across the floor of the communal chamber, her arms out wide, copying the mannequin dancing in front of her. The doll was animated by *Stormlance*, who had quickly discovered that it could use the child's toy as an avatar of sorts. Intended for Manyia to practise her telekinetic interactions, the psychically blank mannequin made an ideal repository for the spirit of Asurmen's ship.

'This was how he used to dance on the Eve of the Fire Ascension,' the ship told them, changing the movements of the doll to a more sedate twirling and bowing, gyrating around Neridiath where she knelt on the floor. 'Twenty of them at a time, changing partners with each turn, the whole party moving like the flames that burned the heavens.'

The mannequin extended its fingerless hand and Manyia bent down to grip the appendage between thumb and forefinger. The two circled each other, the doll with its doughy features split in a wide grin, the eldar child chuckling constantly.

'What are you doing?' Asurmen demanded of *Stormlance*. The ship internally flinched at the chastisement.

Trying to remember what it was like to be you, it replied to Asurmen alone.

'Those are my memories, not yours,' the Phoenix Lord snarled. 'Leave the female and the child alone, there is nothing in them to interest you.'

But there is, insisted *Stormlance*. *Her daughter is nothing yet, but you must sense Neridiath's fear. It fills her, drives her, teeters on overwhelming her. She will break and she will fall headlong into Khaine's embrace. Quite delicious.*

'I will let nothing harm her, and that will not happen.'

Of course, you are their guardian, their protector... She sees through your lies. She knows what we are and hates us, but she cannot deny your demands. I like her. Perhaps she will like me.

'You are distracted,' Asurmen warned. 'There is no love or kindness in you. Stop these cruel games.'

Stormlance pulsed forth a sensor check and the animated doll suddenly stopped and stepped back, lifting a hand to its ear as though listening.

'A problem,' the ship intoned out loud in its sing-song voice. 'It appears that one of the blockade vessels has moved closer than you had hoped.'

'Have they found us?' asked the pilot. Through the ship, Asurmen detected that Neridiath's heart had started to race at the thought.

'Not yet, but we have to enter the atmosphere,' the Phoenix Lord replied, sharing in the data analysed by *Stormlance*. 'That will generate far more heat than we can mask. It will attract attention.'

'Can we not wait until it is safer?'

'No!' Asurmen's conscious thought flowed through the ship. 'Enough of this dallying. I must concentrate on other matters.'

The doll flopped lifelessly to the floor. Manyia started crying, stooping over the inert mannequin, not understanding why it had stopped playing. Neridiath stood and picked her up, smoothing her daughter's hair with her free hand.

Share.

'No, my darling, I've told you, we don't do that any more.'

Share!

The psychic demand was accompanied by a wail so loud that it made Asurmen wince. The child was problematic, but the pilot would never be parted from her.

'Just this once, but this is the last time,' Neridiath conceded. 'You must learn to live within your thoughts.'

The child's lamenting stopped immediately and she looked up at her mother, eyes wide. As their gazes met, Manyia let her spirit free and Neridiath opened up her thoughts to her daughter. There was a moment of connection, of shared love.

Asurmen pulled back, feeling like a voyeur on their affection.

Even as she psychically sheltered Manyia, Neridiath detached a tiny part of herself, trying to latch onto *Stormlance*'s matrix. The ship gently rebuffed her at first. She tried again and the Phoenix Lord's ship responded with a much firmer denial, cutting her off abruptly as though a door had slammed in her face. She was about to try again when the ship addressed her.

'Do not try to share the matrix,' Asurmen said, the lights turning a blood-red in warning. 'This is for your protection. You do not want to associate your spirit with the essence of a Phoenix Lord. Remain in your cabin and play with your child.'

Rebuffed, Neridiath embraced Manyia and lay on the bed with her daughter. Pushing thoughts of them aside, Asurmen enmeshed his will with the thoughts of *Stormlance*.

'You are not like them. Stop trying to pretend you are what you are not.'

And what of you, noble avenger? What are you pretending?

'Silence! You are deluding yourself, yearning for

something that can never happen. You are what you have become, nothing else. You cannot return to innocence.'

They entered the upper atmosphere of Escatharinesh, the ship becoming an artificial meteor with a long tail of white fire. One of the nearby Shards detected them and its flight bays opened, spewing forth a stream of oddly asymmetrical interceptor craft. Like crescent moons tilted slightly on their axis, spiny protrusions jutting at irregular angles from their hulls, the fighter craft ignited plasma burners with flares of orange and red stark against the darkness of the void.

Their course will intersect with ours before we have reached our objective, the ship told Asurmen.

Stormlance briefly shared an overview of their orbital position and that of the crashed battleship. The projected route of the interceptor cloud crossed that of the Phoenix Lord's ship about two-thirds of the way to their destination.

'Is there an evasion course?' Asurmen enquired.

Why would we want to evade them? Do you not want to fight? You've never been cowardly before.

'I must deliver the pilot safely to the battleship.'

A conflict is unavoidable.

Asurmen reviewed the navigational records since they had left the tradeship. *Stormlance* had taken a longer route than necessary to reach the planet.

'You did this on purpose,' he admonished the ship. 'Your hunger for battle could destroy us all.'

After the disappointment of the webway chase, I thought a little action would be welcome. I was getting bored.

The ship arrowed down towards the cloud layer, crossing the terminus from night into day.

IV

Illiathin kept his pace even but lengthened his stride slightly, aware of the tread of feet behind him growing closer. He knew he should not have cut through the Starwalk district. He had left the spire race late, but the opportunity to congratulate Naerthakh Windrunner in person had been too great to miss. Even now Illiathin rubbed his fingers together, remembering the smoothness of the feathers of Naerthakh's wings, a silky blackness like a shroud around the champion racer.

He knew that he could not run. If he ran, it would be weakness, a sign that he was prey. The Starwalk had always revelled in its notoriety, but of late the amusements and distractions promised by its fleshpots and shadowy dens had grown too extreme even for Illiathin's increasingly exuberant tastes. There were rumours that others had come here, from the core worlds, bringing new pleasures, new sensations to be enjoyed. Not only that, they had come with violence, taking much by force that they could not cajole with promises to the mind and flesh.

Bloodletting, the sharing and shedding of life's fluid, was commonplace. Illiathin had friends that enjoyed being bled almost to the point of death, teetering between existence and non-existence, savouring various narcotics in the process. The imbibing of blood was odder still, and there were rumours that not all of the participants in recent times were willing subjects.

The Bloodwalk, some called it. People disappeared, so the whisperers would have gullible listeners believe. Nonsense, of course, Illiathin told himself. As bad as those that claimed the body-swappers and skinshifters had forgotten what it was like to be a normal flesh-and-blood eldar. There was always someone to disapprove of each new pursuit, each fresh stimulant, pastime or indulgence. It was at times as if the doom-mongers of the Exodite movement had never left.

As much as Illiathin dismissed tales of abductions and blood sacrifices, he was never one to take unnecessary chances. He considered cancelling his appointment in the amorous and adventurous embrace of Astriatha, but he was almost through the worst of the district. The alleys would soon broaden into the boulevards and then he would be in the Park of Starwrought Love and amongst normal folk again.

The people behind him were whispering and giggling amongst themselves. Feigning an itch, Illiathin activated his ear implants to filter out the background of raucous music with its pounding percussion and strident wailing, smoothing away the screams of delight and ecstatic laughter.

'We're coming for you, pretty one.'

'Such a tall one, so long to bleed every last drop.'

'Every vein and artery, open you up, drain you dry.'

'Thirsty, pretty one, so, so thirsty. Drink you up, sup, sup.'

Illiathin could hear their excited breathing, the sharp intakes of breath, suppressed moans, the sound of teeth gnashing.

The rasp of blades being drawn.

He tensed, about to run, when light exploded around him from above. It was an airyacht, and behind the blaze of yellow light several figures moved, jumping down into the alley around Illiathin.

The blood devotees hissed and yelped like scalded beasts, retreating into the shadows with arms raised to ward off the blinding illumination. Illiathin's rescuers stepped past him, lifting staves and cudgels as they advanced on the blood-drinkers with violent purpose. They were dressed in bodysuits and tapering helms, clad with chestplates, vambraces and tall boots.

The stalking eldar turned and fled into the darkness, shrieking threats and curses. Illiathin lifted a hand in thanks as his saviours returned.

'I must credit you for your sense of timing, friends. Another moment and they would have been upon me. Good fortune is my companion today.'

'Fortune has abandoned you for some time,' said one of the armoured eldar. He removed his helm, to reveal himself as Tethesis. His hair was cropped short but for a thin braided topknot that fell across his face. The red paint of fake tears had gone, replaced with a black band across his eyes, running from temple to temple. Illiathin *had seen it before, a symbol of a group that called them-selves the True Guardians. Vigilantes, no better than any of the other cults and gangs that had started a hidden but violent war for territory in the city heartland. 'I have not forgotten you.'*

'What are you doing here? Spying on me?'

'Come with us,' said another of the True Guardians. She laid a hand on Illiathin's arm and gently guided him towards the airyacht as the spotlights dimmed to a more tolerable amber hue. The red shafts of lift-beams sprang into life. Illiathin stepped into the light of one, the True Guardians converging around him. There was a moment of weightlessness and then he found himself on a walk-way that ran the length of an outrigger deck along the side of the yacht.

'We can get you out of here, brother,' said Tethesis, appearing in front of Illiathin. 'Passage aboard the Rebirth of Ancient Days. *It leaves tomorrow morning.'*

'A long-distance tradeship? You would send me away on a cargo-hauler? To what purpose? Are you still sore that I would not go with you to that primeval hellhole you wanted to call home?'

'It is not safe here, you must see that.' Tethesis turned and raised a hand. The yacht lifted higher, taking them away from the star-shaped district of walkways and alleys below.

Illiathin looked down, seeing the haze of burning fires and smoke, still hearing the odd scream and shout, a cry of delirious joy and darker roars from crowds watching arena duels and pit races. It had changed so much, so quickly, but it was still the city he had known for all his long life.

'This is my home,' he told his brother. 'How can you ask me to leave it? Are you going?'

'No, we will stay and do what we can to resist the encroachment of the dark ones.'

'Dark ones?' Illiathin laughed at such grandiosity. 'Pleasure-seekers, a few that tread the line a little too often, but dark ones? This is not the War in Heaven, Tethesis. Who appointed you the True Guardians? Whose law do you uphold? You are nothing more than just another group of thugs trying to intimidate and bully your values into everyone else.'

'I will not force you to leave, though I could,' said Tethesis. 'This is my home too, and I will not let it slide into anarchy and self-serving hedonism. Will you join us, brother? Will you fight to protect what remains of our society?'

'I will not,' said Illiathin. 'If you had any sense you would leave these fools to their rumour-mongering and hate-games. You do not have to seek out others to belong, brother. Forget this self-important quest and come to live with me. I know that we have shared harsh words in the past, but I regret them and would make amends. Live with me and we will be a family again.'

'There are still a few more vessels to leave,' was Tethesis's reply. 'You should be on one of them before the end begins.'

'Just take me home,' said Illiathin. 'I ask again as I asked before, just leave me alone.'

13

The column of eldar war machines snaked along the river, anti-grav engines rippling the water as they skimmed silently through the forest. A squadron of Shining Spears Aspect Warriors ranged ahead on their jetbikes while the bulk of the expedition was made up of Wave Serpents and Falcon grav-tanks, supported by a squadron of more jetbike riders and heavy-weapon armed Vypers.

Bringing up the rear, Nymuyrisan and Jarithuran waded their wraithknight downstream, their starcannons at the ready should a foe appear on either bank. It was not an ideal situation for the tall walker, but Hylandris had insisted that Nymuyrisan accompany the task force, claiming that it would not be enough simply to breach the Chaos lines and seize the webway gate, the portal had to be held long enough for the eldar to escape from both the City of Spires and the *Patient Lightning*. Grav-tanks were superb on assault, but they needed to use speed and manoeuvring to fight at their best – traits hampered by the need to defend a static position.

Nymuyrisan could understand the farseer's concerns, but he could not shake the misgivings that emanated from Jarithuran's spirit. His twin had always been the more cautious of the two, and flooded the wraithknight with an aura of reluctance.

'It's better this way,' Nymuyrisan told his brother as they strode around another loop in the broad river. 'Would you rather we stayed in Niessis getting shelled?'

An image flashed through Nymuyrisan's thoughts: the forest around the battleship ablaze with war.

'The *Patient Lightning* is the least of our worries at the moment, you know that. Once Hylandris has secured the *Ankathalamon* the webway is our most secure route off the planet. We have to hold the City of Spires and we have to retake the portal. There is no point defending a crashed ship that has no pilots.'

Sorrow permeated the wraithknight, accompanied by a scene of mourners clad in white hooded robes parading through the Resting Grounds of Anuiven.

'That's unfair. Hylandris offered us all a choice, and he spoke plainly of the risks. Tynarin chose to come on this expedition as much as we did. Or have you forgotten that we volunteered for this duty?'

Regret and the mental equivalent of a sigh.

'We took the decision together. Just as we did everything else. Every path together, until the end.'

A memory rose up from Jarithuran, one that Nymuyrisan knew well. He saw his brother, clad in the purple-and-black armour of an Anuiveneth Guardian, manning a distort cannon alongside Nymuyrisan. Mortar shells from the human trenches rained down around them, their blasts getting closer as spotters zeroed in on the battery of support weapons defending the flank of the advancing eldar. Jarithuran was urging his brother to move, but Nymuyrisan would not heed him, his focus on an armoured transport that had just broken from the humans' lines.

'You swore forgiveness, but still you bring up that moment whenever I do something you don't like,' snapped the wraithknight pilot. 'I've given up the rest of my life to be with you, sacrificed an existence outside of this walking wraithbone tomb to assuage my grief, and you still think I need reminding of what happened?'

His protest was ignored and the scene continued to unfold as it had done countless times before. A mortar bomb landed in front of the d-cannon, showering Nymuyrisan with mud and flame, throwing him to the dirt. Out of the corner of his eye he saw the distort cannon platform tilting over, its anti-grav engine whining to keep it level. The weapon fell across Jarithuran, pinning his legs. His dismay did not last long as a second bomb detonated, making a ruin of both the d-cannon and Nymuyrisan's twin.

'Do you think I would not change the past if I had the means? Why do you torment me when we have far more pressing matters to keep in mind?'

The view switched, so that Nymuyrisan saw through his brother's eyes, that last moment before death engulfed him. He was shocked to feel relief, a gladness that it was him and not his twin that was dying.

The shock was so profound that Nymuyrisan almost fainted. The wraithknight stumbled, falling to one knee in the water. Cocooned within the crystal circuitry at the heart of the giant machine, Nymuyrisan regained his composure while Jarithuran stood them up.

'You've never shown me that before, why now?'

The image froze in Jarithuran's thoughts, a plateau of fire and whirling shrapnel, Nymuyrisan clambering to his hands and knees, a hand outstretched to his beleaguered twin. It was heart-wrenching to relive that moment yet again.

Finally Nymuyrisan understood his brother's meaning.

'You are afraid that I am going to die? Have no regard on that account – why else do you think I joined you in this artificial body? Of course I am going to die, in battle, in bloody fashion. We should have fallen together, both consumed by the hunger of war, but we did not. Do not think I have a life to give without you, it is merely an extension of empty existence.'

A communication from Lathiedes, the Exarch of the Shining Spears, intruded upon their exchange.

'As we feared, the enemy have the portal, held in strength. We approach, draw out their counter-attack, and then strike. Follow us, be ready with your weapons, and stay strong.'

The grav-tanks accelerated away from the wraithknight, water pluming as grav-engines whined to full power. There was a moment of unconscious agreement between Jarithuran and his living twin. The dead pilot pushed the wraithknight towards the left bank of the river. As they forged onto dry land, water streamed from the elegant limbs of their war machine.

The snap and thunder of battle erupted in the distance. Nymuyrisan felt his brother's reluctance and pushed it away with a flood of impatience.

'Run, now!'

The wraithknight broke into a sprint, feet churning up the soft earth of the riverbank, branches that stretched over the waters bending and snapping as the tall walker powered past. As the river meandered lazily to the right and widened, the banks steepened on both sides, forming cliffs that rose above the trees, cliffs atop which the humans had prepared their first line of defence.

Jetbikes and grav-tanks sped back and forth, unleashing beams and blasts that scoured the tops of the cliffs. In reply heavy weapons chattered and boomed, hurling bullets and shells down into the water, each cliff-side battery covering the opposite riverbank.

Slowing the wraithknight, Nymuyrisan took stock of the situation, bringing up the scattershield as anti-tank guns on the promontories adjusted their aim, their shells falling around the margin of the water not far from the eldar walker.

The Shining Spears and Vypers had pressed on, riding the gauntlet of fire to break through to the webway portal a short distance beyond the cliffs. The Falcons were doing their best to lay down suppressing fire on the clifftop positions, while the Wave Serpents were falling back, searching for a flatter part of the bank on which to disgorge the Aspect Warriors they were carrying.

Jarithuran set the wraithknight into motion even as Nymuyrisan only became conscious of his agreement with his dead brother's plan. The scattershield sparked and flared from incoming fire as some of the humans diverted their attention away from the grav-tanks on the water, but the wraithknight pushed through, sending up short bursts of plasma from the starcannons.

Heading into the forest a short distance, using the bulk of the nearest cliff as a shield against fire from the opposite shoreline, the wraithknight stopped beneath a rocky outcrop. The glowing field of the scattershield folded back on itself as Nymuyrisan cut the power, boosting all of the energy he could to the legs and arms. Under Jarithuran's guidance the eldar war engine reached up for the first handhold.

The rock held and they climbed, gaining speed with Jarithuran's increased confidence in the stability of the cliff face. On a couple of occasions they had to traverse sideways to seek large enough hand- and footholds, and just beneath the summit there was an overhang to negotiate. Hanging seven or eight times its own height above the trees, the wraithknight was suspended only by wraithbone-cored fingers for several heartbeats, swinging from side to side until the left foot found purchase on a ledge. With a last surge of wraith-energy the walker heaved itself over the lip of the cliff.

As Jarithuran crouched them to one knee, Nymuyrisan activated the scattershield again, covering almost the entirety of the humanoid war engine. The starcannons opened fire over the glowing edge of the energy field, carving furrows of blood and molten metal through the machine guns stationed on the waterside edge of the cliff.

The Flesh-thieves were strangely unmoved by the appearance of the monstrous wraith engine in their midst, a few of the heavy weapon crews turning their fire against the behemoth, the rest continuing to rain down fire on the tanks below. With its shield still held forwards, the wraithknight straightened and advanced, the detonation of plasma blasts from the starcannons setting fire to gun pits and fighters in cowled robes, vaporising flesh and improvised barricades with crackling blue fire.

From here it was possible to see the gate itself. It was formed from three curving spires of rune-etched stone, each twice as tall as the wraithknight, forming a pyramid structure in a clearing along the bank of the river. It was dormant for the moment, the grass between the portal stones clearly visible, as were the trees beyond. There was a lot of activity around the psychic pylons, boxes stacked close to the gateway, garlands of twisted cables stuck to the gate towers with bubble-like globules of an unknown adhesive substance.

'Are they trying to activate the gate?' Nymuyrisan asked. 'Is that why they came, not for the *Ankathalamon* at all?'

'No matter. Motives are unimportant, need remains,' replied Lathiedes. 'Drive them out – the gate must be ours again. Show no fear.'

Jarithuran guided the wraithknight to the edge of the cliff, kicking aside the remnants of an archaic-looking field gun. The plasma-scarred corpses of its crew burst under the tread of the war engine but Nymuyrisan paid little heed to the sensation. Fire from across the river shrieked over the water, lighting up the scattershield. A few bullets that passed the energy field sparked harmlessly from the wraithknight's armoured form. Below, squads of Aspect Warriors forged into the forests, seeking routes up to the opposite clifftop. Attack craft circled overhead, ready to swoop down in support of the eldar assault.

Nymuyrisan sent a volley of plasma along the cliff, driving back a platoon of humans taking cover amongst the scattered rocks and bushes.

'Push on to the webway gate, we have you covered fro–'

Nymuyrisan's communication to the task force was cut short by the eruption of a huge fireball. The detonation engulfed the whole warp portal. Flame and smoke spiralled into the sky, wreathed in purple and blue psychic lightning. Shards of crackling ghost-stone sprayed into the sky, burning with white flame. The explosion caught dozens of Flesh-thieves in the blast too, the shockwave hurling their shredded bodies out into the river.

The huge detonation left a burning crater where the webway portal had been, burning trees and fragments of gateway pylon spewing black and blue smoke. Almost immediately the call for a withdrawal spread across the communications network.

'I don't understand, why did they destroy it?' asked Nymuyrisan. He let loose a salvo of plasma fire down towards the ruined gate, to cover the Falcons retreating from the water's edge.

An image flashed through his thoughts from Jari-thuran, of a piece of meat on a steel trap.

14

Despite the incredible speed of atmospheric entry it was still some considerable time before they would reach the battleship. Asurmen had picked their entry point to maximise the distance between them and the orbiting Chaos ships, minimising the chances of being detected whilst in open space. The sudden change of position of one of the vessels had rendered that plan unnecessary but it had been too late to make any significant alterations.

As the gap between them and the interceptors narrowed, *Stormlance* was able to conduct a more accurate scan of the incoming attack craft. Asurmen felt the presence of a semi-living essence as he had in the larger vessels – Splinters from the Shards – but there were also clearly human crew manning the interceptors. Two pilots were located near the top of each crescent-shaped hull, alongside three gunners, each manning an energy-based weapon system. The Splinters were approaching at top speed, but as they closed their power distribution shifted, moving from propulsion to manoeuvring and weapons.

They look agile. The tone of *Stormlance* indicated that the ship relished the prospect of the imminent fight. Asurmen had to agree with the assessment if not the sentiment. There was something in the way the interceptors moved that put him in mind of a pack of cruel predators.

The ships broke into three squadrons, eight craft in each, one moving higher and the other two splitting to come at *Stormlance* from the left and right simultaneously. The eldar ship countered by diving straight down, plunging through the thick cloud layer below. The interceptors adjusted, turning as they swooped, though unable to match *Stormlance*'s rapid descent.

They levelled out just below the cloud, a windswept sea stretching beneath them. In the far distance was a coastline of jagged rocks and soaring cliffs, which quickly heaped up into hills and mountains, at the heart of which the battleship had crash-landed.

Stormlance ascended once more, the gravity drive pushing them to the vertical in a few heartbeats. Asurmen did not interfere. It was better if his spirit-shard controlling the ship was left free to do what it did best: kill.

Again the Splinters moved to follow, having to spiral upwards to match the climb of the eldar ship.

As I'd hoped, they do not possess inertia dampeners, the ship remarked. *Their manoeuvring is curtailed by the physical limitations of the crew.*

'So we should be able to avoid them more easily?'

Avoid them? No, it means it will be much easier to shoot them down!

'You are enjoying this too much.'

I enjoy everything I do, I cannot be otherwise. My destruction is of no concern, this is only the latest of many physical incarnations I have controlled. It is only a mortal cloak, destined to end at some point. You know this better than any other. You made me what I am.

Asurmen felt mounting unease as *Stormlance* sped towards the enemy fighters, in direct contradiction to the bubbling undercurrent of elation and expectation that was coming from the ship. It was strange to look in upon himself in this way, and he wondered if this was what others witnessed when they saw him in battle. The feelings of delight ebbed and flowed, as if the ship sang to itself at the prospect of violence, and Asurmen understood briefly how Neridiath felt when confronted by the warlike nature of the Phoenix Lord.

It was her influence, her presence on *Stormlance* that was colouring his perspective of the fight. Her distaste for conflict, her fear of it, was leaching into his thoughts, distancing him from the spirit-piece controlling *Stormlance*. It was not often he was afforded such a vantage point, to see part of himself in this way, and he did not like what he saw.

Closing fast with the enemy craft, *Stormlance* fired first, rolling left while it unleashed a burst from its dorsal pulse laser. The lead ship of the enemy squadron exploded into black smoke and flame, remnants of the greyish-silver hull spinning into the cloud below. The thrill of excitement from the eldar ship was almost like a delighted squeal in the Phoenix Lord's thoughts. He felt a counter-impulse of disgust from Neridiath.

Ignoring her revulsion, *Stormlance* adjusted course.

Turning onto a new target, it fired the keel pulsar, a spray of white energy bolts cutting through a second enemy fighter.

There was a moment of static build-up that crackled across the sky and then the remaining Splinters of the opposing squadron returned fire. Purple lightning streamed across the gap, but *Stormlance* had already started its evasive manoeuvre, pitching the nose down hard, the crackle of the discharges dissipating some distance above.

The second squadron was turning in behind *Stormlance* as the first broke formation, the surviving interceptors peeling away from each other to fall after the rapidly descending eldar ship. *Stormlance* switched trajectory, pulling up tightly into a loop that brought them in behind the pursuing Splinters. Pulsars sprang into life from both mountings, destroying two more.

Asurmen fought against the surge of elation that greeted the destruction of each fighter craft. He reminded himself that each blossom of flame and shrapnel was the death of five living beings, even if they were only humans. The fact that they were Chaos-tainted, already the Lost, was something to be lamented, not celebrated. It was hard to maintain discipline in the face of *Stormlance*'s exuberant satisfaction.

Despite these early successes, the enemy were everywhere. *Stormlance* veered and climbed, rolled and dived, purple lightning bolts screaming past the sleek starship with each turn. A twisting roll powered the eldar vessel up through the middle of one of the attacking squadrons, seeking to use them as a shield against the other fighters. The Chaos-enslaved crews had no compunction about opening fire close to their comrades and lightning followed *Stormlance* through the climb, catching two of the enemy craft in crossfire. The energy blasts scattered across the hulls of the strange craft like water droplets on granite, but some unseen damage was delivered and the afflicted Splinters dropped out of the sky like stones.

You value their lives more than they do, it seems. The eldar craft seethed with the joy of killing. *That changes the rules, doesn't it?*

'This is not a game!' Asurmen was fighting himself now, feeling his subconscious control of the starship slipping further and further away. He was not sure why the ship was so defiant. Like an unruly steed trying to throw him, *Stormlance* rebuffed Asurmen's psychic impulses with a mental laugh.

Then came the realisation that *Stormlance* was feeding off the sense of vengeance deep inside Asurmen's spirit. The Splinters were part of the Shards, and the Phoenix Lord's guilt at not having destroyed them was manifesting as an overwhelming urge to destroy them now.

The Phoenix Lord could feel the cloud of enemy fighters all around them, looping and circling, gradually closing in like a net around the eldar ship. They took no evasive action, but came straight at the eldar, three more falling prey to the pulsars while the trap closed. Asurmen reasserted his will, trying to snare *Stormlance* in a cage of restraint and discipline.

'It does not look like their morale is failing. Cease this disobedience and break away, you cannot hope to destroy them all.'

I do not need to.

Stormlance reversed its gravity drive and for a moment

Asurmen felt the world turning upside down, the manoeuvre too extreme even for the inertia dampeners. A flash of pulsar fire destroyed another Splinter and a second later they were plunging back towards the cloud cover, a dozen fighters turning sharply after them.

As it inverted, the starship extended its scanners towards the battleship crash site. The air was filled with other craft, eldar in design – nightwings, hemlock wraith-fighters, crimson hunters, all launched from the *Patient Lightning*.

I told you not to worry. Our friends are on their way.

The Chaos craft were clearly outmatched, but there was no pause in their pursuit as *Stormlance* led them into the wave of eldar aircraft. The air blazed with lasers, missiles streaking past on trails of blue fire. Into the teeth of this storm swept the Chaos fighters, oblivious or uncaring of the danger.

Asurmen felt *Stormlance* slowing, about to turn.

'Break away!' The command was accompanied by a whip-crack of anger that hurt the Phoenix Lord as much as it chastised the ship. It had the desired effect, and *Stormlance* was cowed once more, continuing towards the crashed battleship.

During the first pass of the eldar attack, half the Splinters were turned into clouds of expanding fragments, leaving smoking ruin and clouds of burning gas across the sky. *Stormlance* accelerated again, dipping towards the battleship that could just be seen in the distance, at the end of a burned swathe through the forest beneath them.

Rather than continue to pursue their prey, the Splinters looped around even as the eldar fighters did the same, determined to engage. The two flotillas hurtled towards each other again, and as before the eldar were superior, losing only one of their number to the lightning cannons of the foe, while only two interceptors survived the exchange.

'Why do they not withdraw?' Asurmen could not imagine what compulsion the Dark Gods had laid upon their followers to make them throw away their lives so pointlessly. 'The battle is lost.'

Perhaps they are not fighting to win.

If that was the case the last two crews of Chaos worshippers were granted their wish, as a swarm of eldar aircraft converged on them with a blaze of firepower that was momentarily brighter than the sun. All that remained as the attack craft parted was a haze of vaporised matter from which molten globules fell like rain.

Asurmen could not suppress a moment of relief, a feeling that skirted dangerously close to satisfaction. He quelled it in an instant, aware of the dangers any amount of gratification might bring. He tried hard to lament the passing of the hunters but could only muster a vague regret that they had not broken away when they had the opportunity – the wanton manner in which they had hurled themselves to their doom made sympathy impossible.

V

Illiathin tried to push his way against the flow of people but he was a leaf on a tide, washing him further and further from the pinnacle conveyor that led up to the star port. Anti-grav engines whined overhead as people took anything that could reach orbit, the sky filled with ascending stars like a meteor shower in reverse.

It was hard to fight against the panic. It seeped into his thoughts, projected by hundreds of eldar around him, like a fungal bloom bursting into life as it spread from person to person, feeding and strengthening and feeding some more.

He had no idea what had caused the surge away from the harbour hub, but he could hear screams and the occasional crackle of energy weapons discharging. He stumbled over bodies, crushed by the press, but corpses no longer surprised him, nor drew comment from anyone else. The apparent ease with which death could come upon someone was the main reason for the crush surrounding the ascender spire.

The stampede lessened after a while, the panic subsiding and the weight of bodies lightening as more people drifted away from the mob, and distance from the threat eased everyone's fears. Despite this, Illiathin could still feel the undercurrent of horror that bound the crowd together, the shared experience of daily fear that shrouded the city like a fog. He let the slow migration continue to carry him back towards the arena park, until he spied a black-suited figure over the heads of the crowd.

She stood at the top of a set of steps to a doorway, a black band across the eyes of her masked red helm. Couched in her arms was a sunfire rifle, and her head moved to and fro, scanning the crowd for any threat.

Pushing his way out of the throng, Illiathin made it to the bottom of the steps, to find the sunfire rifle pointed at him.

'Get away from here,' the guard barked, her voice amplified by her helm. 'Move away or I'll disintegrate you.'

'I need your help,' Illiathin called out.

'Everyone needs our help, but it's too late. Get away before I shoot you.'

'You're True Guardians, yes? My brother, Tethesis, he's one of you. You have to get me to him. Get a message to him. Tell him that Illiathin is sorry. I'm sorry I doubted him.'

'Tethesis? He's never mentioned a brother.' The guard paused, communicating by some other means. After a few moments she took a step forward and offered him a hand. 'It seems that he's the forgiving type. Come inside.'

The door slid open behind her, revealing a narrow hallway. Another member of the True Guardians, his helmet off but still garbed in black body armour, came down the corridor to meet him. Illiathin followed the silent guide through the tower. Lanterns lit the interior with pockets of blue and green light. Power supply was sporadic, as it was across most of the city while vying factions and political groups swapped, bartered and fought for control of the world's infrastructure. Contact with many other worlds had been lost altogether, especially the Core. The last visitors and transmissions had been from craftworlds fleeing carnage and mayhem. There was even word that world fought against world again, as in the days of Ulthanash and Eldanesh.

A spiral stair took them up level after level, the climb starting to tire Illiathin's long legs. They reached a spire-top mezzanine. There had once been a garden here, growing across the balcony that encircled the tower just below its tip; the dead remains of plants were draped over pebble pathways, brown and drab against grey stone.

Tethesis was speaking with some other eldar, variously pointing down to parts of the city and gesturing up to the overcast sky. The guide signalled for Illiathin to stay where he was and crossed the roof to announce their arrival. Tethesis looked over and nodded before sending away the other eldar.

'I really thought you were dead, brother. I looked for you near the arena, but everyone said you had been taken by the blood-drinkers.'

Illiathin said nothing but laughed and cried at the same time, joy, relief and fear all bursting out of him as he stumbled into an embrace with Tethesis. They parted after a moment, looking at each other. Tethesis had a scar running from his left cheek to his neck. It looked strange to see such a physical mark of violence. Not so long ago it would have been a matter of moments to remove the blemish, but now the best medical facilities were in the hands of the warlords who had risen up to claim control of the world.

'We need to get to the Twilight Voyager,' said Illiathin. 'It is the last ship in orbit, and none will return. The craftworld is our last chance to get away from here.'

'It's too late,' said Tethesis, sighing. 'The ship has already departed. There was a riot and the crew broke the moorings. Thousands died. We had people at the station.'

Illiathin staggered back as if struck, chest tightening with dread. Tethesis came after him, a steadying hand on his shoulder. Taking swift breaths, Illiathin fought to control the sudden panic. He could see across half the city from this height, far past the arena and into the central districts. Many of the buildings were in ruins, a blot of smoke seeping up from their remains. Even now he could see the flash of las-fire and imagined the zip and crack of weapons, the clash of blades, the snarls of fighters competing for dominance.

Out there were those that did not care, in their thousands, caught up in whatever exotic and esoteric pursuits and pleasures dulled them to the madness that had engulfed the eldar people. The world burned around them and they cared nothing for its demise, only to sate whatever thirsts and hungers gnawed at their hearts.

Thinking about it made Illiathin's head hurt. There was more to his discomfort than physical tension. For some time he had felt a strange pressure, an overwhelming burden that made his limbs leaden and fogged his thoughts. At times he would lose all sense of himself, of the world, unable to move or think. Like now, he often felt as if he were a puppet, under the sway of some greater power.

'You feel it, don't you?' said Tethesis. 'I gave you warning. We said this would happen.'

'What would happen? What is happening?'

Tethesis held a hand to the side of his head and looked skywards, his gaze far away.

'Our doom. It is coming.'

15

The news that the Flesh-thieves had destroyed the web-gate added an even greater sense of urgency to the task laid before Hylandris. If the followers of the Dark Lady were no longer trying to claim or guard the portal, they would attack the vault in greater numbers. On hearing the news the farseer had made a quick calculation and come to the conclusion that he had little over half a day before the enemy forces departing the webway portal would reach Niessis.

Most of that half-day had now passed without result. He had to release the *Ankathalamon* before sundown and dusk was fast approaching.

'If only your scrying was a little more accurate, perhaps you could have foreseen yourself entering the opening code,' said Zarathuin, peering over Hylandris's shoulder as the farseer bent over the vault's locking mechanism.

'And perhaps I should smash your head repeatedly into the lock in the hope that will break it,' the seer snarled in return. He straightened and glared at the warlock, though the ghosthelm hid his expression. 'Do you take a perverse pleasure in pre-empting my failure?'

'No,' said the warlock. 'There is nothing perverse about it. You are a thoroughly arrogant, unlikeable boor. Seeing you fail would give any normal spirit a sense of happiness and justice.'

'Your craftworld will die,' the farseer pointed out.

'All things die,' the former philosophy tutor replied airily. He stepped past Hylandris and examined the runestone-studded lock pedestal. 'It's a shame our ancestors were so paranoid, otherwise we could just blast open the vault doors and be done with it.'

'Your speculations are...' Hylandris paused, considering his companion's words. He returned his attention to the lock. 'They are unintentionally insightful. Perhaps there was a point to keeping you around.'

'What do you mean? We can't possibly destroy the doors with the firepower we have to hand. We could call in the wraithknight, I suppose, but there's bound to be a defence system, perhaps even a world-destroyer.'

'Quieten your prattling, I'm thinking.'

Zarathuin fell thankfully silent while Hylandris considered the problem with a fresh perspective. He spoke his thoughts aloud, the vocalisation demanding greater clarity and precision, which helped him move purposefully from one idea to the next.

'The *Ankathalamon* was buried here at the end of the tsinnin extermination. Nobody thought it would be used again. The tsinnin were all dead, every last pod and larval drone. Nobody thought the world would be colonised by ignorant humans an aeon later.'

'And nobody would steal a weapon that can only affect one planet,' added Zarathuin, following the seer's line of thought. 'Security measures would be minimal. Perhaps a few psychomaton guards and a tamper warning system.'

'And a straightforward locking cipher.' Hylandris jabbed a combination of rune-forms into the locking mechanism, hope rising as each stone lit up in turn. A faint sigh echoed through the chamber as the vault doors parted a hair's breadth. 'Or perhaps even a straight-forward coda from the Miseries of Vaul! Trusting times, my friend, unlike today.'

Now that the device had come to life, Hylandris could feel the psychic web that controlled the whole vault. Unlike the infinity circuit of a craftworld or the matrix of a starship, there was no energy pulsing along the crystal conduit. The psychescape felt cold and barren as Hylandris eased his mind into the unlocked apparatus, his mind exploring the disconcerting emptiness as though his thoughts echoed inside his own head.

'Farseer, the humans are in sight.' The message came from Kahainoth, leader of the rangers Hylandris had persuaded to his cause. 'Armoured vehicles leading the way. Countermeasures are in place but we will not be able to stall them for long with the weapons we have.'

No need to engage them, we almost have what we need, Hylandris replied. With a small exertion of will, he broadcast his message to the small host that protected him. *All forces are to withdraw at once from the City of Spires. We have what we came for.*

'A little presumptuous?' said Zarathuin.

'Not at all,' said the farseer. Another extension of

psychic power flooded the vault with energy. Crystal geometries and runes sprang into life on the walls and doorway. A simple command was all that was required for the vault doors to swing outwards, revealing their prize.

The vault was not much larger than the antechamber, with a dome a little higher than Hylandris was tall. The scalloped crest of his ghosthelm almost scraped the ceiling as he entered. As he stepped across the threshold lights glimmered into life, revealing six shadowed alcoves around the circumference of the chamber. Turning to the right, Hylandris walked the perimeter of the room, moving from one alcove to the next, assembling the *Ankathalamon* from each component in turn.

When he was done he had circled to the door. He held his hand up to Zarathuin in triumph, a bracelet about his wrist connected with fine golden chains to emerald rings on two of his fingers.

'The *Ankathalamon*!' the farseer declared. 'The Fate of Nerethisesh incarnate. The power to raze all life from a world.'

'Is that it?' Zarathuin peered at the device. 'That controls the life-destroying systems of Nerethisesh? A dull piece of jewellery? I was expecting something... grander.'

'It is a key, nothing more. With this I will activate the purge systems of Nerethisesh, wiping out the humans that have grown like mould on our lost world. The Imperium in its ignorance will respond, casting their blame on the fools of Ulthwé. Eldrad Ulthran will be far too busy dealing with that threat to meddle in the affairs of Anuiven any further.'

Zarathuin grabbed the farseer's arm, jaw clenched.

'That was not the plan you explained to me when we set out on this quest,' said the warlock. 'We were to deny the Chaos worshippers access to the *Ankathalamon*.'

'You are an idiot, Zarathuin.' The farseer pulled his arm free. 'No human could master the psychic subtlety required to breach this vault or employ the *Ankath-alamon*. The presence of the Flesh-thieves is entirely coincidental, an easy guise for my mission. I have no idea why they are here if they are not seeking to break into the webway.'

'You have betrayed our trust,' Zarathuin insisted. 'The war between Anuiven and Ulthwé was to be fought between unwitting proxies, but now you risk the madness of the humans being unleashed against any and all of our kind. And you should know better than to dismiss coincidence. It is not chance that brought the Flesh-thieves upon us, but their mistress. She has a reason for being here, even if we cannot guess it yet.'

Hylandris pushed past the warlock and strode to the transport capsule. He stepped inside and turned.

'Your years of philosophy have weakened your resolve. Moral absolutes are the refuge of the insecure and pathetic. We must be strong or our craftworld will fall.'

Zarathuin hesitated before following Hylandris onto the conveyor. The protective field closed around them, and in moments they were ascending to ground level. It was a short distance to the outer portal, but the humans were already pushing along the valley floor, tanks and armoured walkers leading the advance.

Not far away Kahainoth and his five fellow rangers waited astride sand-and-red camouflaged jetbikes, two more of the anti-grav steeds hovering alongside them.

Shells began to detonate against the pillar of the vault, showering grit and dust down onto the eldar.

Hylandris broke into a run as the rumble of tracks and growl of engines grew louder. The first armoured vehicle in the human column trundled around a rock column not far away. Dragging up his robe to his thighs, he swung a leg over the jetbike's saddle and grasped the handlebars. He checked over his shoulder that Zarathuin was mounted. His companion avoided the farseer's gaze.

'Let us leave this Isha-scorned place,' Hylandris said, signalling for the group to head off.

Engines whining, the jetbikes lifted higher and accelerated away, leaving trails of disturbed dust, abandoning the City of Spires to the incoming tide of the Flesh-thieves.

VI

Staggering through the streets, Illiathin clutched his head, trying to push away the pain that throbbed behind his eyes. He stumbled into someone and rebounded into a wall where he slumped, looking up at a blood-red sky. He slid down the wall to the ground, still staring up at the heaving tempest overhead.

The sky looked back at him, glowering with malign intent. The swirl of the storm clouds looked so much like an eye that Illiathin flinched, turning his head to avoid its gaze.

He tried to summon the will to stand up, to keep moving, but after a half-hearted attempt fell back to the ground. He moaned as the pressure inside his skull returned, making it feel as though his head would burst.

Illiathin peered across the street and saw a young eldar maiden weeping, her clothes shredded to rags, her face and arms bleeding from dozens of scratches where she had clawed at herself with broken fingernails. Others had been more extreme. Many of the True Guardians had killed themselves rather than endure the creeping paranoia that had swept through the populace.

Illiathin sat up when he felt the ground tremble. At first he thought it was the shockwave of an explosion, but the vibration did not stop. The sky was growing darker and darker, the blot across the heavens that had swathed sun and stars alike for many days was expanding, growing, coming closer. At first he had thought of the storm as besetting Eidafaeron alone, but the horrific realisation had dawned that the apparition was immense, truly cosmic, engulfing the entirety of the core worlds and the systems beyond. The doom swathed the entire eldar empire.

There were fresh screams from nearby. Wails and cries of sorrow and pain.

He realised he was shouting too, on his knees, weeping as he held his hands out to the sky to placate the descending Doom. He tasted blood on his lips and lifted a finger to his face. It was coming from his nose.

With a last effort he managed to get to his feet and limped a few steps, swaying from side to side as the ground shook. Forlorn, he stopped in the middle of the street. A handful of other eldar were close by, paying no heed to each other, mesmerised by the violent display in the heavens.

Looking up, Illiathin had a strange sense of vertigo. The broken towers loomed over him but it felt as if he looked into a deep abyss. There was a glimmering light at the bottom, growing brighter, coming closer. Entranced, he watched the light approaching, squinting when it became too bright.

The ground bucked, flinging him from his feet. He

smashed his head, fresh blood pouring from the wound. Groggy, Illiathin rolled onto his front. The light was every-where now, seeping through the shattered windows, leaking from doorways, engulfing the whole world.

The light and the pressure inside his head were one and the same. His mind had been a candle and now it was an inferno, trying to break free from the puny shackles of his will.

More screams echoed along the street, so high-pitched he thought they came from some animal. The maiden who had wounded herself was shrieking, battering her head against a wall, her movements jerky and uncontrolled.

She turned suddenly, her face mashed, splintered bone poking through ripped flesh as she stared at Illiathin with insane eyes. For a moment her seizure stopped.

Everything went still. The ground ceased its movements and the light was all-suffusing. The ambient glow made everything a vague ghost at the edges of Illiathin's vision.

The sky split with a crack of thunder multiplied ten thousand-fold. Light burst from the maiden's eyes and open mouth. An undulating aura of gold and silver poured out of her in a stream, lifting like wind-blown motes into the sky.

Illiathin saw others likewise afflicted, faces turned sky-wards, their spirits rippling in a shining thermal from their bodies. From across the city, from all across the world, across all of civilisation, the essence of the eldar was ripped from their bodies.

The spirit-stuff coagulated, becoming a seething cloud of psychic energy that roiled and burned and screamed inside Illiathin's head, as though he were both part of the storm and watching it. Something monstrous thrashed and howled at the heart of the cloud, straining, snarling, pushing to break free.

The spirit-stream ended. The empty carcasses of the afflicted eldar toppled to the ground like dolls dropped by some obscenely powerful child. Illiathin stood rooted to the spot in abject terror as he felt the deaths of billions of his people. A background psychic chorus of life that he had taken for granted since birth, suddenly silenced.

Everything else, everyone else, had gone. He felt utterly alone for the first time ever.

And then the universe broke apart.

16

Neridiath had expected to find the stricken battleship half broken, lying amidst its own wreckage at the centre of a ploughed furrow of destruction. She was surprised to find nothing of the sort.

The eldar vessel was in the middle of a clearing, supported by the lower two of its four fin-like solar wings, the prow touching earth that had been cleared by the scorching entry. There seemed to be little external damage that would prevent take off once the anti-grav engines had stabilised the horizontal trim. Whoever had been piloting the ship had done a remarkable job, and Neridiath thought that perhaps the task in front of her was not so daunting as she had imagined.

The *Patient Lightning* was the largest vessel Neridiath had ever been aboard. The launch bay that swallowed up *Stormlance* and a flotilla of escorting attack craft could have housed the *Joyous Venture* with room to spare. Asurmen's ship came alongside a quay about a third of the way from the inner wall, sliding gently to a halt above the docking platform. An arcing bridge linked the quay to the floor of the bay, where a small group of eldar had gathered.

Most of the fighters peeled away, returning to whatever duties they had been performing before the appearance of Asurmen's vessel. Neridiath watched them go, Manyia peacefully asleep in her arms.

We should not keep our hosts waiting. Asurmen's voice drifted across the matrix from elsewhere on the ship. *Matters are rapidly approaching their conclusion.*

Neridiath reached out mentally and caught the briefest glimpse of a small chamber, lit only by an ambient twilight that came from dozens of tiny motes floating freely. Asurmen's armour was stood to one side, but there was no sign of the Phoenix Lord. Suddenly the lights disappeared and Asurmen's armour straightened, the lenses of the helm glowing green with internal energy. The shock of the change broke the connection, leaving Neridiath with a pounding heart, her breath coming in shallow gasps.

We have docked, the ship informed her. *I hope to spend time with you again.*

'That will never happen,' replied Neridiath, thinking of how the starship had so gleefully put them all in danger.

The door opened, a gesture for Neridiath to leave. There was the faint glimmer of psychic power and Manyia stirred, blinking open her eyes and yawning.

Goodbye.

Neridiath said nothing, but hurried out of the chamber, eager to be away from the contrary vessel. Asurmen was already at the tip of the boarding bridge. She was struck by his statuesque appearance. She had literally seen that pose in statues and paintings and other works for as long as she had been alive. A moment of fancy took her and she wondered if her likeness would be immortalised for her part in the continuing legend of the Asuryata. She had to admit to a certain thrill at the thought. Few were chosen to be agents of Fate.

Asurmen looked round at her approach and Neridiath felt a brief surge of impatience from the Phoenix Lord.

'Have I kept you waiting?' she replied with a scowl, her enthusiasm waning as they neared the point of action. The threat of battle was starting to loom large in her thoughts and her petty sarcasm masked her growing dread. 'Perhaps you feel that I have inconvenienced you in some way?'

Ignoring her barbed remarks, Asurmen set off down the incline to the waiting group below. Neridiath followed a few paces behind, taking stock of the welcoming committee. She saw three robed seers, two in the rune armour of warlocks, a third wearing the high-peaked ghosthelm of a farseer. A small system of runes circled about the farseer's torso and head like satellites, glinting in the setting sunlight that stretched into the launch chamber.

With the seers was a short, slender eldar dressed in an extravagant chequered body suit of red and dark blue, over which he wore a long coat of soft white fur trimmed with scarlet cloth. His hair was braided in a complex knot that hung past his shoulder, gems glittering in the golden bands that held it in place. She knew his type immediately – corsair captain. She had thought the *Patient Lightning* part of the Anuiven fleet but it was obvious that it was actually crewed by outcasts. She wondered if that boded well or not.

The last member of the group was an eldar so old that his skin had started to thin, veins clearly visible like ink seen through stretched parchment. He wore light robes hung with several talismans that identified him as a bonesinger – the constructor-mystics that could weave objects out of the psychic plastic known as wraithbone. He was ancient, and his presence confused Neridiath even further. The bonesinger was clearly accomplished in his field, and most of his kind with such experience stayed aboard the craftworlds creating new artefacts and ships, but here he was fulfilling the role of engineer on a pirate ship.

'I am Hylandris, of Anuiven,' said the farseer, stepping forward. He half turned, about to introduce his companions when Neridiath interrupted him.

'I've heard of you, Hylandris the Star-breaker! To claim you are of Anuiven would be for me to say that I am Isha, simply because I have seen her statues. You are an outcast. Worse, a renegade.'

'Our new arrival knows you too well, Hylandris,' said one of the warlocks. He raised a hand in greeting, the other kept on the hilt of the Witchblade that hung at his belt. 'I am Zarathuin and the other warlock is Faeriunnath. We are most definitely still welcome members of the Anuiven community, I assure you.'

'Do we really have time for these introductions?' Asurmen said. 'The pilot is here, we should take off as soon as possible.'

The outlandishly dressed captain grimaced.

'Our rangers and jetbike squads warn us that the Flesh-thieves are about to mount another offensive. We are most vulnerable in the first moments of lift-off and we cannot risk doing so while under direct attack. Their longer-range cannons have been silenced, but they still have many guns to threaten us. We must repulse this assault before we can leave.'

'It is as I foresaw,' added Hylandris. 'Rest assured that when the moment is upon us, we will act.'

'You choose strange company,' said Neridiath, turning her accusing stare on the corsair. 'I assume this is your ship?'

'Tynarin Tuathein, void prince, known by many as the Brightness of Heavens,' the captain said with a sinuous bow. Neridiath found his manner skirting between sincerity and mockery and was taken aback by his disarming smile when he straightened. 'This is the *Patient Lightning*, and you have my eternal gratitude if you can save us from this deplorable predicament.'

'Basir Runemaster,' the bonesinger said curtly. 'I owe you no explanations. Repairs are ongoing, but we are not yet ready to leave.'

'You are the pilot, yes?' said Hylandris, stepping in front of the others to reassert his authority. He looked at Asurmen. 'I had foreseen her arrival. You, I did not expect.'

'Do not be hasty to hunt a single future,' the Phoenix Lord said quietly. 'Lest in turn the future hunts you.'

'Is that a threat?' said the farseer, stepping back. He cast a glance at the two warlocks, as though they might intervene on his behalf.

'We are here to protect you from the Dark Lady and her minions, nothing more,' Zarathuin said. 'Did I strike you as insane? I am not challenging a Phoenix Lord.'

Tired.

'You all need to stop talking,' Neridiath told them sharply, hoisting Manyia a little higher. 'Someone is going to tell me exactly what I need to do, but if we are not leaving right now I need somewhere for my daughter to sleep.'

'It will be better if you are also rested,' added Asurmen. 'The task ahead will be taxing in the extreme.'

'Our oversight, madam Neridiath,' said Tynarin, interposing himself between the pilot and Hylandris. 'Follow me to your quarters. The *Patient Lightning* is rather large, best that you do not roam without a guide.'

Neridiath nodded and followed as the captain turned away, beckoning for her to accompany him. Asurmen was at her side and the others were close on her heel. She turned her head and looked up at Asurmen.

'It seems to me that everyone is very busy making sure I know exactly where I am supposed to be,' she said.

'You are very important, it is only concern for your safety,' the Phoenix Lord replied.

'Yes, I'm sure that's exactly what it is.'

When they reached the passageway adjoining the launch bay Basir Runemaster muttered some excuse and left them, heading aft. Hylandris dismissed Zarathuin and Faeriunnath, explaining that they should move to counter the enemy incursions towards the battleship. With a growl, Zarathuin excused himself and stalked away, followed by the other warlock.

'Are you not fighting with them?' asked Asurmen.

'I'm a seer, not a warrior,' snapped Hylandris. 'Besides which, I am too valuable to the craftworld to risk my life in close confrontation.'

'Just exactly what is your role here?' said Neridiath. 'You

were outlawed from Anuiven a long time ago, what concern is it of yours what happens to the craftworld? And speak plainly, I'll take none of your enigmatic seer mystic-speak.'

Hylandris paused in his stride for a moment, apparently insulted by the implication. He knotted his fingers together at his waist as he started to walk again, and spoke without looking at Neridiath.

'The son never forgets the mother. I accept that some of my activities might be seen as meddling in the lives of individuals, but recent events have proven I was right to pursue my studies in the direction I did. Anuiven is under threat, and I am helping divert that threat back onto its perpetrator. It is my intent to redirect the forces currently besieging this battleship, so that they will interfere with the expansionist plans of Ulthwé.'

'You are setting yourself against another craftworld?' Neridiath was equally amazed and horrified by the notion. 'These depraved humans will kill other eldar?'

'A regrettable but unavoidable consequence to a conflict initiated by the seers of Ulthwé. It is they that have placed Anuiven in danger to protect themselves. I am simply responding to their aggression.'

'And the seer council of Anuiven backs your actions?'

'Their interference is undesirable,' the seer confessed. 'They know of the ongoing crisis. They will be grateful for my intercession on their behalf.'

'I don't understand how this squabble can be a threat to all our people,' the pilot said to Asurmen.

'There are consequences to every decision, reactions to every action,' the Phoenix Lord said. 'What begins as strife between two craftworlds can extend to all. The war cannot be allowed to escalate.'

'Well said,' exclaimed Hylandris. 'If we can head off this altercation now, it shows Ulthwé that they are not above retaliation. They will stop turning events against Anuiven and we can continue in peace and companionship.'

'How do I have anything to do with this?' asked Neridiath. She touched a hand to Tynarin's arm. 'What happened to your pilots?'

'They were wholly subsumed within the navigational matrix when we suffered a catastrophic energy reverse.' He hesitated, grief passing across his face. 'Their minds have been burned out. Only their physical shells remain.'

'How did the starship not crash? Fate has spared you a catastrophic end.'

'The *Patient Lightning* used the last vestiges of its conscious minds to steer itself to safety,' the captain said. 'We could take off, but without a pilot like yourself to mesh with the matrix, we cannot hope to outmanoeuvre the ships waiting for us. The spirits that drive us are simply unable to understand or even perceive such material matters. Those cursed ships would cut us to pieces before we even broke orbit. Do not concern yourself, the ship will do the fighting, you just have to lend it your nervous system.'

Neridiath wasn't sure what to make of this and kept the rest of her questions to herself. The more she found out about what was happening, the less convinced she was that she should be involved.

They stopped in front of a golden archway sealed by ornately decorated doors. The doors swung open at Tynarin's command, revealing a transport chute. The captain darted a look at Hylandris and then Asurmen, before waving for Neridiath to board the transporter.

'We should allow our guest to rest before we tax her with more lengthy explanations,' the corsair said when she had stepped aboard. He moved into the doorway, blocking the entry of the others.

Asurmen looked at Neridiath. 'The task at hand is to blunt the next attack of the Flesh-thieves. The moment we are ready for take off, you must be ready.'

'Try to relax and rest,' added Tynarin. Neridiath gave him a dubious look. 'Please try.'

'We have a battle to wage,' Asurmen told the others, turning away.

'You mean a battle to win,' said Hylandris.

'Possibly.'

The doors closed soundlessly, leaving Neridiath and Manyia alone with the corsair captain. He smiled as he passed a hand over a control panel, impelling the transporter to the destination they needed. With a gentle hum the conveyance set into motion.

Strangers.

'Farseers and Phoenix Lords and pirates,' whispered Neridiath, under the guise of kissing her daughter's forehead. 'Strangers indeed, my little starlight.'

Danger?

'Sleep, beautiful one, and never worry about that.' She cast a glance at Tynarin, who was feigning disinterest, closely inspecting the gem of a ring. 'I won't let anything happen to you.'

VII

Illiathin ran, carving swirled furrows through the glittering gold fog that had descended on the city. Everywhere he looked were dead bodies, strewn along streets and alleys, some hideously broken where they had fallen from upper floors and balconies. All had disturbingly peaceful expressions, as though in their final moments their anguish had been taken away, their worldly desires satiated at the point of death.

A cackling laugh broke the stillness, betraying the presence of other survivors. Knowing the manner of eldar that had ruled the city in its final days, Illiathin had no desire to encounter these others.

He ran towards the headquarters of the True Guardians, his mind a whirl of conflicted thoughts. Fear for Tethesis drove his legs to move even though his mind was in numbed shock. Fear for himself propelled him also, fuelled by a sliver of hope that his brother survived and would protect him.

The fog started to coalesce, forming larger and larger droplets. Shining silver beads the size of his fist slowly drifted to the ground, sliding through the air like tears running down a cheek.

Astounded, Illiathin stumbled to a stop. He held out his hand and one of the droplets fell into his outstretched palm. It was cold to the touch at first, but after a heartbeat of contact it warmed up, seeming to leech life from Illiathin. Not leech, he realised, but share. The droplet hardened in his grasp, becoming an oval stone. It pulsed quickly, the rhythm matching his speeding heart.

There were other stones around him, settling on the floor. He grabbed as many as he could, putting them into the pockets of his robes, filling two pouches that hung at his belt. He noticed that these others remained inert at his touch.

As he straightened from collecting another, he looked up, seeing the sky for the first time, the mists now little more than a glimmering wisp in the air.

He dropped the stone in his hand, a silent scream locked in his throat as he saw what had become of the heavens.

The sun burned black in a magenta sky, its surface contorted with whorls and ripples like agitated oil. Around it a crown of stars was arranged, glimmering diamonds of white light that slowly orbited. Beyond, the stars of the deeper sky winked in and out of existence, some of them burning red and green and blue, others fluctuating wildly, phasing in and out of reality.

The sky itself shifted and swelled, like a wave just before it breaks, distorting the star field even further. It made Illiathin dizzy to look upon it but he could not tear away his gaze.

Turning, he surveyed the sky all around, his stare coming to rest upon two pillars of fire that burned in the void, huge conflagrations of yellows and orange despite the vacuum of space. He realised that they were the columns of the webgate consumed by psychic energy, once vastly distant but now impossibly close.

Illiathin managed to drag his stare from the heavens and started running again, panting in desperation, eyes scanning the broken buildings around him for a sign of the familiar streets he was seeking. Now and then he glimpsed someone in the distance, at a far junction or on an aerial walkway above. Some stood in shock, others were running too, some staggered fitfully in stunned horror.

Eventually he found the True Guardians' headquarters. The guard at the door was dead, an orb of crystal settled on his armoured chest. Leaping over the body, Illiathin dashed through the open door. The dead were in every room and corridor within, slumped against the walls, lying headfirst down the spiral stairs, collapsed across chairs and tables and work counters.

He found two people on the roof, staring up at the sky.

'Tethesis?'

One of the armoured figures turned and relief flooded through Illiathin at the sight of his brother. The two of them staggered towards each other, so numbed by events they could neither laugh nor cry.

A sudden explosion near the centre of the city drew their attention. A column of lightning speared upwards, white and purple, coruscating into the heavens for several heartbeats. In its wake it left a slash across the sky, which at first Illiathin took to be an after-image in his eye. But the crack in the air did not move as he turned his head. Black smoke seemed to pour from the rift, heavy, boiling down into the narrow streets and alleys of what had once been Starwalk.

The tear grew wider, suddenly expanding to engulf several more towers with violent bursts of energy.

'A warp rift,' muttered Tethesis. 'A wound on reality.'

'There's another,' said the other True Guardian, an eldar called Maesin. She pointed to a rainbow of fire that sprang from the arena park, its arch slowly flowing outwards. Beneath the span of bright colours was a shimmering plane of black and gold.

'What is it? What has happened?' asked Illiathin. He lifted up one of the sky-tears he had found. 'What are these?'

Tethesis took the proffered stone and like the first that Illiathin had found it sprang into life at the touch of his brother, glowing a deep red in his hand.

'It seems to be psychically keyed,' offered Illiathin. He showed his brother his own stone. 'Can you feel it? The connection?'

'I do,' said Tethesis. He gestured for Maesin to take another and the three of them stared in marvel at the glowing crystals.

'The old world has ended,' Tethesis declared. 'This new world contains many perils and miracles. In time we will learn about them, but for the moment survival is the key. Others have survived, and they will not all be allies.'

'We are damned,' Maesin said quietly. 'The doom that was prophesied has come to claim us and this is the hell we have built for ourselves. Hearken to the cries of our tormentors.'

Illiathin listened, but it was not the sporadic shouts and cries from the streets that Maesin referred to. There was a whispering, a constant monologue on the edge of hearing, of threats and promises and descriptions of unspeakable acts. The more he listened, the more Illiathin was convinced that the voice was his own thoughts. He lost himself, caught up in the taunts and temptations.

Tethesis's hand on his shoulder broke the bewitchment. Illiathin looked out over the city and saw darkness and madness, the stars above reeling and wheeling like drunkards, the sky itself broken and torn. Beyond, he could feel something else, something that was part of him, that was joined with his spirit at the most fundamental level. It was monstrous and malign and it was aware of him, desiring Illiathin's essence for itself.

Illiathin fell to his knees and buried his face in his hands, trembling violently, terrified beyond comprehension.

17

The Flesh-thieves attacked at dusk, amassing all their disparate forces for the assault on the battleship. It began with a storm of shells that made the ground shake, ripping gouges through the forest, turning the flattened clearing around the crashed starship into a wasteland of smoking craters. The eldar had no choice but to withdraw from the hellish deluge of shells, surrendering the approaches to the ship to escape the bombardment.

Splinter-craft from the Chaos cruisers in orbit flitted across the darkening sky, lighting the twilight with flares of lightning from their cannons. The sleek shapes of eldar aircraft moved effortlessly through the descending enemy squadrons, taking a heavy toll. On the upper decks of the *Patient Lightning* point-defence blisters sprang into action, unleashing torrents of converging laser fire to destroy and drive away the incoming attack craft. Explosions blossomed across the ruddy cloudscape and shattered fighters fell like rain, but a few of the

Chaos craft managed to break through. They ignored the battleship and sped across the burning forest unleashing incendiary bombs that drove the eldar even further back. They were eventually hunted down by the eldar fighters or caught by the gunners aboard the downed battleship.

Amidst the blazing of shells and flaming detonations the wraithknight of Nymuyrisan and Jarithuran crouched under an overhang of rock, as much power as they possessed fed to the scattershield. The white flare of the energy field was lost among the destructive barrage, just another bright flash of light. Even so, shrapnel and earth pattered against the armoured skin of their war engine, midnight-black with tiger stripes of purple almost invisible in the dusk.

The tempest of destruction ceased as soon as it had begun. The boom of detonations and scream of diving aircraft had gone, replaced by the crackle of fire and the throaty roar of crude combustion engines. The whirring of motors and screech of sawn wood was added to the din as armoured walkers led the ground assault, chopping down trees with spinning saw blades and ripping them from the ground with energy-wreathed fists. Behind them came more stumpy war engines, lumbering forward on short legs as they unleashed volleys of rockets from pods on their back.

Though much of the covering terrain had been flattened or set afire, the eldar moved back into what shelter they could find. The eldar targeted the walkers with starcannons and brightlances, the dark, scorched remnants of the woods lit by the flare of lasers and plasma. In the dance of shadows squads of Striking Scorpions advanced, their chainswords and pistols at the ready.

On the open ground around the battleship the Falcons, Fire Prisms and other grav-tanks slipped forwards, turrets turning as they unleashed bursts of anti-tank fire at the incoming enemy. The walkers pushed into this barrage of fire, armour pierced and torn open by bolts of plasma and blasts of azure laser. Fuel tanks exploded in gouts of fire and black smoke, adding to the already hellish nature of the scene.

Along paths cleared by these mechanical brutes came the tanks and infantry carriers, bumping and labouring over broken stumps, sliding down the sides of craters, tracks churning dirt and ash. Behind them marched even more humans, clad in a mixture of robes, padded jerkins, soldiers' uniforms and plates of solid armour. Each bore in tattoo, scar or daubed symbol the rune of the Dark Lady, the mysterious champion that had amassed such a grievous host.

The Chaos-tainted were intent upon the battleship, uncaring of the casualties being inflicted by the flicker of scatter lasers or the pulse of starcannons. Swooping Hawks flitted above the advancing mass on their winged flight packs, snapping off volleys of fire from their lasblasters. Weaving between return fusillades of las-bolts and bullets, they launched haywire grenades at the tanks, overloading engines and more sophisticated systems with bursts of electricity and electromagnetic discharge. Plumes of plasma from dropped grenades followed wherever the winged Aspect Warriors moved.

Giving no heed to providing themselves with covering fire or protecting their flanks, the Chaos horde pushed on towards the *Patient Lightning*, directly into the teeth of the eldar defence. In silence, Nymuyrisan watched as a squadron of tanks and a platoon of infantry advanced past no more than a stone's throw from the wraith-knight's hiding place, ignorant to its presence.

When they had passed, Nymuyrisan wanted to surge out of their cover and attack, but his instinct to fight was baulked by refusal from Jarithuran. The dead twin kept them crouched where they were, resisting his brother's insistent mental commands that they move.

'We have them at our mercy!' Nymuyrisan complained, flooding the wraithknight's spirit circuit with disapproval. 'We should attack now!'

There was no response from Jarithuran, just an obstinate silence and no reaction from the wraithknight. Irritated, Nymuyrisan tried to override his brother with sheer force of will, urging the walker to rise and attack. The command faded into nothing, dissipated by Jarithuran's obstinate opposition.

The battle continued to rage as Nymuyrisan watched with frustration. A dozen tanks had been reduced to burning wrecks, at the cost of a trio of eldar vehicles. The toll amongst the Chaos infantry was impossible to calculate – hundreds already, possibly thousands. They cared nothing for the carnage, their vehicles ploughing through piles of the dead, the soldiers that followed clambering over the wounded and slain without hesitation.

It was only then that Nymuyrisan realised why Jarithuran had waited.

Behind the infantry attack came an immense machine, towering above the tanks and transports. It advanced on six mechanical legs, crushing the remains of tanks and warriors without trouble, the few remaining trees in its path shouldered aside with splintering trunks. On its back was a turret mounted with two huge cannons.

It paused in its approach, all six legs locking firm to provide a firing platform. The turret tracked from right to left, following a target. With a thunderous boom it opened fire.

A bright apparition screamed across the battlefield – to Nymuyrisan experiencing the battle through the wraith-sight of his war engine it appeared as a pair of flaming skulls. The psychically charged rounds hit a Fire Prism and exploded with green fire, shattering the hull of the grav-tank. The remnants flipped and tumbled over and over, cutting a swathe through a squad of Guardians that had been manoeuvring their distort cannon into position behind the tank.

The behemoth started forward again, secondary weapons in a score of turrets opening fire, trails of tracer rounds and the detonations of explosive bolts shining in the darkening twilight. A squad of Swooping Hawks dived towards the hulking war engine but were met with a hail of fire from cultists manning anti-air weapons mounted on cupolas on the creature's spine.

Like a door being opened to admit a gale, Jarithuran suddenly allowed Nymuyrisan's impulse to inundate the wraithknight's psychic matrix. The war engine leapt into a run, driven by the pilots' desire, the starcannons spitting plasma at the Chaos behemoth.

Closing on the huge monstrosity, Nymuyrisan was taken aback for a moment, almost losing his balance. The thing they attacked was not simply a machine, there was flesh beneath the armoured flanks and turrets, dark blue and scaled. What he had taken for a vehicle was an armoured beast, its horned head sheathed in a metal helm that he had taken to be a driver's compartment.

He recovered his wits quickly enough when the turret swung towards them. Activating the scattershield, he brought up the left arm a moment before the Chaos followers manning the beast opened fire. The skull-shells punched straight through the shimmering field and smashed into the scattershield generator. Jade flames licked up the arm of the wraithknight and the scattershield hub exploded with a cloud of sparks.

'This could be problematic,' said Nymuyrisan, but Jarithuran was paying no attention.

The wraithknight, fuelled by the dead twin's anxiety, accelerated to a sprint, the starcannons falling silent on its shoulders. Large-calibre bullets and phosphorescent shells whipped and cracked past the charging war engine, the occasional strike doing little to slow the wraithknight's progress.

They slammed into the side of the Chaos beast at full speed, dipping one shoulder. The impact lifted up the behemoth as the wraithknight's legs straightened. Nymuyrisan gasped at the weight but he was almost a bystander, his brother's fury powering their actions. Feet sinking into the dirt, the wraithknight pushed and pushed until three of the beast's legs were off the ground.

The behemoth tried to get away, but the wraithknight grabbed an armoured plate, the metal twisting and buckling yet holding firm as Jarithuran sought to flip over the bucking beast. Top-heavy because of the turret on its back, the behemoth could do nothing as the wraithknight straightened to its full height and lifted.

Like an upended turtle, the beast rolled over. The turret

crumpled beneath the weight, the sorcerous ammunition within exploding with a series of blinding blue, red and purple detonations that showered both beast and wraithknight with murderous scythes of serrated splinters.

A piece of gun barrel speared through the chest of the wraithknight. Nymuyrisan gave a shout and Jarithuran's anxiety sent a flare of reaction through the matrix. Focusing on the behemoth, Nymuyrisan took control, grabbing the beast's helmed head and pushing it aside to expose a mottled yellow throat. The ghostglaive shimmered with psychic energy, a ripple of fire dancing along its length. Nymuyrisan plunged the blade into the behemoth, sawing through its thick skin and muscle.

A dozen Chaos cultists had survived and were ineffectually shooting at the wraithknight with pistols and lasguns. Rising again, the eldar walker swept half of them away with a sweep of the ghostglaive. The others Jarithuran incinerated with a volley from the starcannons.

Standing over the defeated behemoth, Nymuyrisan was panting hard, as though the exertion had been physical rather than mental. He was thinking of a humorous observation to share with his brother when something smashed into their left shoulder, the impact ripping away the arm and sending the wraithknight spinning down into a spreading mire of mud and behemoth blood. The shot had torn away part of the chest plastron, shattering part of the psychic circuit. Nymuyrisan tried to make contact with his brother, but for the first time since they had been born he could not feel his presence. Physically dazed, the wraithsight of his machine swirling with interference, the pilot turned his attention to what had fired at them.

In the distance a second Behemoth trampled through the woods. The flickering of witchfire could be seen as its cannons aimed directly at the toppled wraithknight.

VIII

Clad in grey rags, Illiathin ascended the steps of the temple, his sack of precious forage over one shoulder. Casting a haunted gaze behind him, he slipped his hand into the hidden recess in one of the pillars of the vast portico, unlocking the small door to one side of the imposing entrance to the shrine. He slipped inside, glad to be out of the ever-present glare that bathed the city.

Bare feet slapping on the stone floor, he followed a narrow corridor around to the main entrance hall. Mosaic tiles underfoot, he cut across the antechamber to the half-hidden stairwell that led up to the priests' chambers. He ascended, muscles moving out of memory more than conscious thought. Dumping the bag on the bundle of sheets that served as his bed, he crossed the chamber to his meagre stash of belongings. Rooting through the frayed and torn clothes, he unearthed two gleaming jewels, one red, the other blue. He clasped them to his chest and fell onto the bed, exhausted.

'It's getting worse,' he told the gems. 'Most have fled into the webway but I fear to follow them. Not only are they depraved, the webway is no longer secure. The daemons that stalk the city have broken the wards that kept the warp separate from the interstellar network. Who can say how much of it is compromised?'

He sat up, the stones in his lap.

'Food is getting scarce. I found fresh bodies by the orchard alongside Raven's Plaza. The remnants of the gangs are fighting over what's left. I can't go out any more, it's too dangerous. I found a passageway beneath the second crypt that leads to the Gardens of Isha on the neighbouring square. There appears to be no taint there, perhaps I will be able to nurture fresh food.'

He stopped, a moment of realisation caused him to stand up, tossing the stones onto the bed.

'What's the point?' he cried out. His voice echoed back to him from the vaulted ceiling of the main shrine, mocking as it diminished.

Illiathin strode to the mezzanine at one side of the chamber, overlooking the temple floor a distance below. Shafts of red light illuminated the temple from windowed domes above. To his left was the statue of Asuryan, rendered in red and grey stone, on one knee, a hand outstretched to his worshippers. From his open hand spilled water into a pool, symbolic of the blessings and wisdom of the lord of the gods.

It was the water that had brought Illiathin here. The temple was defunct, the gods had died long ago during the War in Heaven, but the shrine had been maintained out of duty and respect for the past. Even the looters and desecrators that had ravaged the city since the anarchy had begun had passed it by and the daemons shunned the district of shrines.

Fresh water and shelter. It seemed a fitting benediction from the lord of the heavens, but it was wearing thin. Comfort, company, hope. These things Illiathin desired but did not have.

It was simple enough to climb up onto the stone balustrade, one hand on the wall to steady himself. He looked at Asuryan's stern but caring face.

'Why? Why carry on?' Illiathin whispered. The words disappeared into the gloom. He glared at the statue of the Lord of Gods. 'Show me you still care.'

He stepped off the rail.

Something snared the back of his robe and he swung, crashing into the wall. Looking up, he came face-to-face with a scowling youth. She was probably half his age, but the look in her eyes was ancient. There was grime across her face and the mane of hair that framed it was knotted and matted. Despite her apparent frailty she held his robe in an iron grip. She took hold of him with her other hand and hauled.

He grabbed the rail and helped her, pulling himself back to the mezzanine.

'What's your name?' the girl asked. It seemed an odd question.

'It doesn't matter,' he replied.

'I followed you in, thought it looked safe. You looked safe. That was a very stupid thing to do.'

'Was it?' Illiathin sat up, pushing the girl aside. 'And who are you to judge?'

'I'm Faraethil. And you're welcome.'

'You're not,' he growled back, standing up. 'This is my home, I didn't invite you.'

The girl looked hurt, but turned and left. Illiathin listened to her footsteps descend the stairs and then heard the thud of the side door closing. He turned back to the temple, about to repeat his actions, but he slowed and then stopped as he reached the rail.

Perhaps Asuryan had reached out beyond the veil as he had asked. He thought about the girl, and wished that he had not sent her away. She could have let him fall and taken his few possessions for herself, but had saved him.

He looked back at the bed, to the two gleaming stones amongst the blankets. A sudden wave of disgust welled up inside him – disgust at himself. Billions had died but he had been spared. Many that had survived were the worst of the cultists and hedonists.

But he still lived, and so did the girl. There had to be others who would do something more with the legacy of a whole civilisation.

He returned to his contemplation, the stones in his lap as he stared at Asuryan's noble features. Hope had not returned. This world allowed no hope to flourish.

There was purpose instead.

18

Night had fallen but the tracery of las-beams and glow of flames lit the sky as bright as day. The flickering illumination hampered the humans' night vision but Asurmen suffered no such weakness and strode the battlefield dispatching his foes with cold demeanour. His vambraces spat shurikens that cut down the hapless humans by the score. The few that survived the hail of monomolecular discs were met by the gleaming blade of the Phoenix Lord's power sword – beheaded or eviscerated, all slain by a single stroke.

Asurmen did not understand how so many humans could have come to the world. The ships in orbit were not sufficient to bring such an army. He had to conclude that they had risen here perhaps, emerging from a human population that had unwittingly colonised the ancient eldar world and then been corrupted by the influence of the Chaos gods.

It did not matter how many the eldar killed, there

seemed always to be another deranged cultist ready to take up the fight. The humans battled with little semblance of strategy or cohesion, making them easy prey for the psychically coordinated eldar counter-attacks. But for all their brutish simplicity, they outnumbered the defenders of the battleship by a significant magnitude. Though ten might die for every eldar casualty inflicted, there were enough humans to weather such a storm.

The tanks in particular and the huge armoured beasts were coming closer and closer. Fire Dragons with thermal guns and anti-tank bombs had done their best to support the heavy-weapons fire of the Guardians and the grav-tanks, but inexorably the humans' armoured vehicles were creeping into range. They would soon be able to fire directly on the *Patient Lightning*, and for all that its hull could withstand significant damage, it would only be a matter of time before some potentially fatal hull breach was made by such an attack.

'Hylandris, can you hear me?' Asurmen knew the farseer would be monitoring the communication. 'We cannot hold the open ground. It is a killing zone.'

What do you suggest we do? Sacrifice our only way to leave the planet?

'Where is the pilot? Can you lift off?'

She is still resting, while the last repairs are made.

'Then we have no choice, we have to narrow the field of conflict. Order the army to withdraw onto the *Patient Lightning*.'

They will rain down a storm of shells upon us! We cannot risk such a foolhardy plan. No, you must fight to keep the humans at bay until we are ready to leave. Sometimes fate demands sacrifice.

'We cannot keep back the humans, no matter how many lives we give for the cause. We must draw them onto the starship and use the situation to our advantage. Their vehicles will not be able to follow and their numbers will choke their advance. We must draw them onto the ship and negate their numbers. Now!'

While he waited for Hylandris's next response Asurmen unleashed a hail of shurikens at a gang of humans scuttling past the flaming wreck of a grav-tank to his left. Three of them fell. The others stopped to return fire, but the Phoenix Lord was already running towards them and only a handful of shots sang past him and ricocheted from his armour before his sword ended the lives of the others.

What if they do not follow?

'They will come. There is madness in them, do you not feel it?' Asurmen could sense a churning of emotion that rose from the human horde like the thermals of the forest fire that surrounded them. The air was thick with the stench of Chaos, a scent Asurmen knew far too well. 'They want us dead, nothing more. Not the *Ankathalamon*, not the webgate, not the battleship. Us. We shall be the bait in the trap.'

We cannot leave with humans on board the ship. It is too dangerous.

'We will not have to,' Asurmen said. 'None will survive long. If we do not do this, the *Patient Lightning* will be destroyed on the ground. You must get Neridiath ready to pilot the ship the moment the assault relents.'

There was another pause. In the following few heartbeats of silence Asurmen slew a dozen more humans with blade and shurikens. Their tattooed skin was flayed into tatters like the rags and uniforms they wore. Dismembered corpses lay sprawled in bloody puddles at his feet. Others in the eldar host had followed the conversation and without any overt order or agreement, more than a dozen squads of Aspect Warriors were falling back, the exarchs heeding the call of Asurmen.

Very well. Hylandris's tone was curt, edged with tension. *Lead them aboard and cut them down. I will wake the pilot and have her ready to take off the moment the repairs are complete and the humans thrown back.*

'It shall be done.'

There was no need to issue commands, to marshal the war host with verbal communication. Guided by the farseer, the new strategy passed at the speed of thought through the eldar army, and within moments the holding attacks and counter-assaults ceased, giving way to a rapid withdrawal.

The heaviest weapons fell back first while a cordon of Aspect Warriors and Guardians held the humans, until they in turn could retreat under the supporting fire of Dark Reapers and grav-tanks. The humans filled the void like air encountering vacuum, swarming into a deadly crossfire between the smaller guns of the battleships, the Falcons and encircling squadrons of jetbikes and Vypers. They died by the dozen while Asurmen led the retreat.

Squad by squad they fell back along the boarding bridges that arced down to the ground from the *Patient Lightning*. Broader docking bays in the lower decks of the ship were opened for the grav-vehicles to enter.

And then the gunfire stopped.

The humans surged like a tidal wave, charging up the ramps after their foes. They poured onto the battleship uncaring of what lay in wait for them, spreading into the *Patient Lightning* like poison in a creature's veins.

And then the eldar struck, and the killing started again.

IX

He felt her rather than heard her. His time alone had honed not only his physical senses but his psychic intuition. The new universe was a place of emotion and feeling, a halfway state between the real and unreal. This much he had observed and deduced, watching the world unfurl from the heights of the temple and spending long days and nights allowing his thoughts to wander, his mind to stray as though ascending the dream-tree again.

She ran.

She ran hard, without purpose at first, several streets away. Those that chased were close, filled with the fire of the hunt, their greed and desire burning like a flame that lit the city with its heat.

He let his essence dissipate, becoming one with the city, hearing her panting as she sprinted, listening to the animal-like yelps and barks of the pursuing pack. Her fear was a streak of chill through the winding streets. No matter how much she twisted and turned, doubled back *and looped, they were on the psychic scent, drawn to her innocence, her purity like hounds after blood.*

And it was blood they wanted. Blood and terror. Her blood, her terror.

Most of them had left, retreating into the webway where the daemons were not so powerful. Here in the between world, the half-existence between life and death, the daemons reigned supreme. The city was theirs now and he had let them take it. All but the temple of Asuryan and the Gardens of Isha. They sensed the ancient power here and though the world now resided in their domain the daemons would not approach.

The city they had turned into their pleasure palace – moulding, shaping, transforming the delights of the few remaining inhabitants into torture, overwhelming the senses with debauchery and the raw energy of Chaos.

He had never really thought about the Chaos gods before. They had been a myth almost, a thing from another place. Like the War in Heaven, a half-truth masquerading as a tale wrapped in a legend and a lie.

But now the Chaos gods were horribly, fatally real. Time had brought understanding, of the nature of what had befallen his people. He lived in the heart of the creature they had birthed, a divine retribution on a scale so vast it had swept the galaxy. Even now he could feel it, suckling at his spirit, drawing strength from his life, sustained by the curse of the eldar that resided in his essence.

A god, shaped of perversity and yearning, of fulfilled and unfulfilled desire, of adoration and the adored; spawned by the laxity of a whole star-spanning empire, brought into being by a descent into self-fulfilment so swift and precipitous that none could have known the full disaster of its ending, not even those Exodites that had so long foretold the coming doom.

His thoughts returned to the girl. Her fear had changed, becoming like a spear, guiding her. He felt her intent, to find sanctuary, to seek shelter where she had found it briefly before.

She came to the column where the lock was hidden and the side door opened with a click that resounded through the temple.

Too late. They had seen her, had seen the way into the shrine.

She had brought them to his sacred place, defiled his peace.

He ran down the stairs to confront her, to send her away again, but when he reached the entrance hall and looked upon her terrified face he could not abandon her.

The others came in cautiously, wary of the rarefied air of the temple. The tranquillity confounded them and they approached slowly, sniffing the air like dogs. Clad in scraps of armour and clothing, long blades in their hands, hooks and barbs passed through skin and flesh as ornamentation.

One of them, a female with red-dyed hair stood up in spines, snarled at the two of them, eyes wild with madness and hunger.

'Who are you?' she demanded, pointing her curved dagger at him.

He looked at Faraethil and then back at the witch-leader. 'Asurmen.' The Hand of Asuryan.

19

Manyia would not stop screaming. The *Patient Lightning* rumbled and thundered as shells impacted on the outer hull, and the corridors reverberated with shouts, gunfire and other din of battle. As disturbing as this was, there was something else that distressed the child. The ship's matrix was alive with the thoughts of war, the murderous impulses of the Aspect Warriors, the fear and desperation of the crew. Worse still, the psychic circuitry was being overwhelmed by the crude rage and dull ignorance of the attacking humans, their minds like stones hurled at the glass of the matrix, breaking it with sheer brutality and mass.

The bestial, base desires and impulses of the lesser beings swamped the matrix, the numbers of the humans such that their effect on the psyche of the ship was akin to a tidal wave crashing against a coastal settlement. Neridiath and the other adults could desensitise themselves from the effect, blocking the interface from the

Patient Lightning. Little Manyia had no such defences as the psychic network broke down, barraging her with a succession of terrifying thoughts and savage images.

The corridor was filled with corpses. The Guardians that had been assigned to protect Neridiath were dead, set upon as they had escorted her towards the piloting chamber. Their mesh armour was torn apart by savage weapons, their attackers likewise slain by shurikens and snarling chainswords. With his last breath Faedarth, the squad leader, had opened up the throat of the final human raider. The gory remains of both sides surrounded the pilot and her daughter.

Carrying Manyia in her arms, Neridiath ran, away from the fighting, away from the encroaching nightmare of the human attack. She tried her best to shield her daughter from the effects of the psychic overload, welcoming Manyia into her thoughts, using her own barriers to mask the ruin running rife through the matrix.

She was not sure where she was running to, turning at junctions and following passages at random. It felt like the humans were everywhere. Neridiath allowed her mind to touch the matrix for a brief instant, and realised that the Chaos worshippers were breaking into the ship at several points, allowed to enter by the withdrawal of the warriors. Neridiath did not understand how the humans had managed to break through so swiftly, and why nobody had come to protect her and Manyia.

Harsh voices speaking in a crude language snapped her back to the present. The lights flickered, a sign of approaching matrix interference, and in their strobing the illuminated walls showed hunched, clumsy shadows approaching from ahead.

Manyia was still shrieking and there was nothing Neridiath could do except clamp a hand over her child's mouth and turn around, heading back the way she had come. Her daughter's thoughts were a mess of panic and fear, no single emotion clear enough to detect, just an agony of psychic distress that matched her vocal wailing. Unable to think, her mind bombarded from outside and within, Neridiath staggered from one corridor to the next, flailing through the ship in a desperate attempt to find sanctuary.

This was not the legendary tale she had expected. Life had suddenly become a terrible, tenuous reality. Neridiath choked back a rising terror, sobbing, trying hard not to think of the danger she had brought upon Manyia. Her stomach was so tight with dread that she almost fell. It was no comfort at all that she had brought Manyia into harm's way to guarantee her future. Gritting her teeth, she forced herself to move on, looking for somewhere safe for her daughter. Asurmen had chosen her, and the farseer had seen them victorious. Neridiath focused on that truth, drawing what strength she could from these facts.

An explosion ahead sent a wave of noise and air flooding down the passageway, buffeting the refugee pilot. She was terrified to turn back, but could not go on further, and found herself caught in mental stasis, not knowing what to do.

Just then she felt a soothing presence filtering into her thoughts. It calmed Manyia and eased her worries, coalescing as the mind of Hylandris. The farseer transmitted control and authority, a tranquil pool of understanding amidst the storm.

Follow my instructions and I will guide you to safety.

179

In the brief oasis of calm afforded by the farseer's intervention, Neridiath's desire to get away manifested itself in a more practical form.

'Should I head to the control chamber, to lift off? We can escape the attack that way.'

We are too vulnerable to take off whilst there are enemies aboard and their armoured vehicles can attack us with impunity. A moment of misfortune could send us crashing back down with disastrous consequence. Also, the humans are concentrated towards the prow – it is safer to head down to the lower decks.

Following the farseer's guidance, Neridiath made her way down several levels, past the weapon decks to the storage levels. On two occasions she was forced to double back, forewarned of roaming humans by an impulse from Hylandris. Eventually he deposited her in an empty storage chamber beneath one of the laser cannon arrays.

There are other matters that require my full attention, Neridiath. Rest assured that all is as we wish. The humans were allowed to board so that we could thin their numbers more efficiently. The process of ejecting them has begun. I will find you when it is safe.

The feeling of loneliness when Hylandris had gone was matched by the emptiness of Neridiath's surroundings. The fighting seemed more distant here, though it still swelled and pulsed across the matrix, a background discordance that Neridiath avoided.

She sat down on the bare floor, Manyia in her lap. The baby was no longer screaming, but her thoughts were a whirl of agitation. Neridiath stroked her hair and whispered comfort, accompanying the physical reassurance with mental projections of safety and calm.

A sudden clatter from the corridor snapped Neridiath from her bonding trance. Footfalls approached, many of them, too heavy to be eldar. Human voices, unintelligible, barking out every few heartbeats. The matrix was awash with their thoughts, of loot and destruction, just as the faint internal breeze brought the stench of their unwashed bodies through the door of the storage chamber.

Neridiath was frozen with dread, her sanctuary violated against all expectation. There was nothing she could do, her shelter had become a trap. She desperately looked around the room but there was nothing to hide her or Manyia. The floor and shelves were bare.

She eased herself to her feet, sliding her back up the smooth wall, moving sideways so that she could not easily be seen through the open door.

A moment later the first of the humans stepped into view. It had bare legs and arms, neck to thigh covered with a thick tunic tied at the waist with a broad belt. Its flat face was sallow, eyes a sad brown as they turned towards the storage bay. Its head was topped with an unkempt thatch of black hair, greasy. It stank of oil and exhaust smoke combined with a rank bodily odour.

Manyia whimpered, loud enough for the intruder to hear. The male turned, eyes widening with surprise as it met Neridiath's panicked gaze. The human opened its mouth, issuing a series of grunts and growls to its companion as it stepped across the threshold. Another followed, a step behind, of darker complexion, head hairless but with a growth of black curls on its chin.

Neridiath realised what she should have done the moment she had heard the humans.

Door shut! Lock!

The ship responded instantly to Neridiath's instinctive reflex, the door plates of the storage bay sliding together like an iris, cutting the second human in half. Head, torso and one arm flopped to the floor of the room in a spray of blood and bisected organs, the human's piercing shriek cut short.

The other human turned, mouth gaping in horror. As it moved Neridiath saw that the front of its tunic was open, revealing a chest crudely shorn of hair, a branded mark laid upon the left pectoral. A symbol she did not know in detail but recognised all the same – a rune of the Dark Gods.

The human looked down in horror at the remains of its companion. It wavered slightly, unsteady on its feet, and then vomited, ejecting a stream of bile and half-digested matter onto the floor. Neridiath backed away, though there was nowhere to run, Manyia squirming in her grip.

Retching twice more, the human straightened, slit-like animal eyes turning on the pilot, a lip curling in anger. It barked something, jabbing a finger towards the remnants of the other human, spittle flying from vomit-flecked lips.

Neridiath started to cry, tears flowing down her cheeks, chest wracked by deep sobs.

'Save me,' she whispered. She did not know to whom she pleaded for aid, perhaps the universe itself. She felt very small and alone and foolish all of a sudden. Fate could be as cruel as it was kind; there were no guarantees in life. 'Save us. Don't let this happen.'

Through the mist of grief, she watched the human take a step closer, one hand closing around the grip of a pistol hung on its belt. It lifted the weapon and beckoned her to approach, snapping and snarling in its savage tongue.

There was no power in the universe that was going to let this beast take her child. The pistol was pointed right at her, the demand repeated with greater volume. But even now she could not do what had to be done. She knew she was faster than the human. She could seize the pistol and fire it before the clumsy alien could stop her. But for all that the knowledge was there, the action was not. A terror deeper even than her fear for her child rooted her to the spot.

She saw only one solution.

Neridiath's fingers closed around Manyia's throat, while she told herself over and over that it would be a mercy for her daughter. There was no telling what the humans would do with an eldar child.

Scare mummy! Die!

Neridiath only caught the edge of the burst from Manyia. The full force of the psychic imperative was directed into the human's thoughts, shaped not by language but by primal need. The human reeled back, wincing in pain. Its gaze moved to the child in Neridiath's arms, half horrified, half confused. A trembling hand raised the pistol to its left eye. Manyia's tiny face was set with a deep scowl, toothless gums bared, unfettered psychic energy gleaming in her dark eyes.

Die!

The human pulled the trigger, sending a bolt of energy searing into its skull. It fell backwards, arms flailing wide, head crashing against the floor.

Neridiath watched the human, wary of any movement, but only spasmodic muscle twitches disturbed the body.

Safe?

Manyia started to cry and wriggled around to bury

her face in Neridiath's chest. The pilot's thoughts veered between shock and horror and relief, the three emotions whirling together in an overwhelming mass.

Through the haze she heard the sound of banging on the door. She realised it had started the moment the door had closed, but she had been focused entirely on the human inside the room. It was just a simple storage locker, not barred by a security door or blast portal. It would not take long for the humans to batter their way in.

Safe?

'Yes, safe,' Neridiath lied, eying the pistol that was still in the dead human's grasp.

X

It was pity that moved him, not anger, and in that came his strength. Asurmen was on the wild maiden in an instant, the fingers of his extended hand crushing her windpipe. As she spun to the floor choking, he caught the blade falling from her spasming fingers. He tossed the stiletto to Faraethil and moved to the next cultist, kicking his legs from under him, snatching the sabre from his grasp in one movement.

He had never fought before, with hand or weapon, but it seemed as though his foes moved slowly, his body acting and reacting without thought. He drove the sword into the chest of the eldar he had taken it from and ducked beneath a wildly swinging axe. Pulling the blade free, he turned, lifting the sword in time to block the next blow.

Faraethil hurled herself at the blood-drinkers with a feral screech, bowling over the closest with her charge, stabbing again and again into the female cultist's chest.

Asurmen slid his blade into the gut of another enemy,

considering the killing a mercy, not a sin. He took no pleasure in it, for he had seen in his long meditations that the gratuitous act, the self-satisfaction of achievement had been the downfall of his people.

The anger and hate of his foes made them hasty and clumsy. They hissed and spat and slashed, but all they did was waste precious time and energy. In the moments of their posturing he cut down two more of their number, their blood flicking from the sword to spatter the main doors of the temple. He moved without fear or hesitation, the epitome of calm discipline. In this state it was easy to spot the flex of muscle, the flick of eye, the subtle movements that betrayed his enemies' thoughts. He was reacting before they even knew what they were going to do.

Faraethil had fallen on another cultist, sawing her scavenged blade across his throat. Her fear propelled her, turning her into a wild creature of desperate violence, full of passion and fierce need. She leapt from the corpse, blood-soaked and dripping, tumbling to the floor with another enemy, biting and screaming while she plunged the knife down.

A curved sword missed Asurmen's throat by a hair's breadth as he dodged the attack of his next target. His empty hand grabbed the blood-cultist's wrist, twisting, shattering bone with effortless ease. Asurmen's sword cleaved down, taking the head from the body in one smooth motion.

One cultist remained. He scrabbled backwards through the blood of his dead companions. Crouching, snarling like a chained hound, Faraethil bared her teeth, little better than the eldar she had slain. Asurmen stepped in front of her, blocking her view.

'What are you?' the cultist demanded, the dagger in his hand shaking as he lifted it.

'I am your evils returned to you,' said Asurmen. 'I am the justice your victims cry out for. The protector of the weak. The light in the darkness. The Hand of Asuryan.'

The sword sang as it cut the air.

'I am the avenger.'

20

'Where is the pilot?' Asurmen demanded. There was no reply from Hylandris.

I... I have made a grave error.

'Where is she?'

I thought she would be safe. There was fear rather than regret in the farseer's voice. *I cannot predict every tiny thing. It's impossible. No, she will be all right. I saw us l–*

Asurmen gave up on getting what he needed from the confused seer. He touched his presence to the matrix of the ship, a bolt of silver that sliced through the babble and noise of the humans, seeking out *Stormlance* in the flight bay below. Connecting with the rest of his consciousness residing in the warship he interrogated the *Patient Lightning*, using the bond that had arisen between *Stormlance* and the child. Wherever Manyia was, Neridiath would be close at hand.

He homed in on the child, finding her in a state of panic, after-images of what she had done looping through her mind. Manyia was reliving the moment of contact with the human's filthy thoughts again and again, each time the sudden blankness of death cutting across the mental link. The destructive cycle was also spilling into the mind of Neridiath along the bond the pilot had created to protect her daughter, polluting her thoughts as well.

Detaching from the infant's psyche, Asurmen wove his thoughts into the sensors of the battleship, locating the pair on one of the lower decks. There were around a dozen humans trying to break in through the thin storage-bay door, and twice that number were in the immediate surrounds.

Asurmen ran.

To the humans it must have seemed that the battleship was consumed by anarchy. The fighting spread across every deck; sporadic thrusts and counter-attacks shifted the lines of battle constantly. To the eldar there was nothing further from the truth. Guided in part by the warlocks and partly by the ship itself, the war host methodically dulled the initial impetus of the human assault and then proceeded to splinter the attacking force with misdirection, carefully conceived counter-attacks and deadly ambushes.

Asurmen navigated through the firefights and whirling melees without stopping until he found the nearest conveyor shaft. Summoning the transport pod he rode the conveyor down to the level where Neridiath and Manyia were trapped. He was deposited in an adjoining corridor, exiting the travel pod directly in the path of a group of humans coming around a corner ahead.

He was already moving before they raised their

weapons. Hasty las-fire flashed down the corridor, too poorly aimed to hit its target. Asurmen tucked into a roll beneath the fusillade, launching a volley of shots from his vambraces. The shurikens sliced down the closest two humans, their robes and flesh left equally tattered as they fell to the floor.

Coming to his feet, Asurmen fired again, his volley slashing open the face of a third foe while the other humans tried to track the swift-moving Phoenix Lord. Las-bolts sparked along the wall in front and behind but none found their mark.

His diresword in hand, Asurmen reached the humans at full speed. The gleaming blade parted the head from the shoulders of one while a point-blank hail of shurikens tore the guts from another. Without a break in stride, Asurmen spun with sword outstretched, severing the spine of the last human. He was already around the junction before the body hit the deck.

The humans battering at the door of the storage bay were so fixated on their goal that they spared no attention on protecting themselves. They howled and bayed like a pack of feral beasts, hammering at the door with fists, rifle butts and the pommels of their knives and swords.

Three fell in quick succession when Asurmen reached them, limbs sheared away with a flurry of strikes. The door gave way as a fourth fell, ribs splayed open by the Phoenix Lord's next blow. Over the heads of the humans he could see through the broken door, to where Neridiath was cowering against the wall.

Seeing her stricken, realising that they had all been a heartbeat away from a terrible doom, Asurmen unleashed his deepest fears and anger, channelling an ire that had lasted for an age.

His blade became a whirlwind of gleaming fire, opening up arteries and severing limbs in a blur of motion. The humans turned sluggishly, finally realising the threat in their midst, faces slowly contorting with shock as the Phoenix Lord carved through their number. Corpses fell from his presence like scythed crops, showering the passageway with arterial crimson.

As the last but one of the humans collapsed, his legs cut out from beneath him, the survivor turned his pistol on Asurmen. The Phoenix Lord grabbed the man by the throat and lifted while the human pressed the muzzle of his weapon against the side of the Phoenix Lord's helm. With a mental command, Asurmen unleashed a storm of shurikens from his vambrace, pressed into the human's chin. The cultist's head disappeared.

Tossing aside the body, Asurmen stepped up to the door, a slick of red washing past his feet.

'Neridiath!' He tried to reach out with his mind but the pilot recoiled from the bitterly cold touch of his thoughts.

Asurmen was about to try again when he sensed something changing in the world. The barrier between realities was thinning. A tear ripped across his consciousness, accompanied by a psychic wailing. Looking down at his bloodstained hands, he finally realised what the humans had been fighting for.

They had been fighting for the Dark Lady. Their lives, thousands of them, sacrificed in her honour. The eldar had been only too willing to shed so much blood. Blood that had been promised to the Dark Gods of Chaos, and every body marked with a symbol of devotion. How could they have been so blinded to the truth?

The Dark Lady had provided her side of the bargain. She was about to receive her reward.

XI

The rage emanated from Faraethil like waves of heat, filling the antechamber with its oppressive presence. Asurmen held his ground as she turned her angry gaze upon him, the blood-drenched knife in her hands dripping crimson across the small tiles of the floor. As before her hair was a wild, unkempt mass, a physical representation of the aura of emotion that surrounded her.

Making no sudden movements, Asurmen slowly crouched and laid his sword on the floor. He stood again with equally deliberate motion, keeping his eyes fixed on Faraethil. Hands spread wide, he spoke softly, his voice barely more than a whisper.

'They are dead. We have slain them. The danger has passed.'

Faraethil's gaze flicked to the corpses and back to Asurmen. Her eyes narrowed, but the hand holding the dagger lowered slightly.

'You remember, yes? You saved me. And now I have saved you. Why did you come back to me?'

The girl slowly straightened, limbs quivering. She sucked in a deep breath and exhaled it, eyes never moving from Asurmen.

'You called yourself the avenger, the Hand of Asuryan.' A hint of a smile played on Faraethil's lips. 'For me. You took the name for me?'

'Your inspiration. You were the instrument of Asuryan's intervention, now I have become the instrument.'

'You know that the gods are dead, right?' The girl looked down at herself and reeled at the sight. She staggered to the wall and threw up.

Asurmen moved to her, close but not so close that she would feel threatened. The knife was still in her hand, after all. Faraethil looked back past him to the bodies.

'Did we do that? Did I do that?' She looked horrified. 'How? How could we?'

'It is in all of us, that violence, waiting to be unleashed. Just as the yearning for delight, for adulation, for satisfaction is in all of our hearts. We must resist its lure, be strong against its temptations.'

'Have you done this before? The killing?'

Asurmen shook his head.

'I was a vessel, nothing more. The violence is in me, but I am a being of serenity now.'

'Really?' Faraethil laughed without humour, staring at the bloodied carcasses of the cultists. 'Serene is not the word that springs to mind.'

'Violence is an intent, not an act,' said Asurmen. 'I have thought long about this, since the Fall.'

'The Fall? What is that?'

Asurmen waved a hand towards the doors and to the vaulted ceiling of the entrance hall.

'Everything that happened. The loss of innocence. The damning of our people. The doom that came.'

The girl looked at him with suspicion. 'You remember the time before?'

'How can you not?'

'I was a child, I don't remember anything except the death and screaming. My brother survived for a while, looked after me long enough for me to learn how to look after myself, avoid the cults and the daemons. It has been some time, several years of the old reckoning, since I was last here. Have you been alone all that time?'

'For far longer than I had realised,' said Asurmen. He gestured to the blade in Faraethil's hand. 'Let me take that.'

She gave it to him, hesitant, and he threw it away, the metal clattering across stone tiles.

'How am I supposed to protect myself!' she cried, taking a step after the discarded blade. Asurmen held out a hand to stop her.

'It is not safe for you to carry a weapon yet. Your rage will get you killed. It blinds you to danger, fuelled by your fear.'

'So you are not afraid? Really?'

'I have seen the world consumed by a thirsting god, Faraethil. There is nothing left to scare me. I have spent enough time alone. Let me teach you what I have learnt, of the world beyond the cults and streets. Let me help you control the fear and anger, to bring calm to the turmoil in your heart.'

'I will have to fight. Nobody survives without fighting.'

'I did not say you will not fight. I will teach you to fight without the desire for it overwhelming you. Our people have been laid low by our emotions, and our desires and fears have consumed us. Those of us that can must learn control. We must walk a careful path between indulgence and denial. We must not pander to our darker passions, but we cannot deny that they exist. Both must be tempered by discipline and purpose. Only then can we be free of the burden of ourselves.'

The girl looked at him, hope and gratitude in her eyes.

'Is that true? Can we really escape this nightmare?'

'Would you like to try, Faraethil?'

'I need another name. You were not Asurmen when we first met. If I am to be reborn, like you, I need a new name.'

Asurmen thought for a while and then a smile turned his lips, something that had not happened for a long time.

'I will teach you to channel your rage into a tempest of blows that none can withstand, and your scream shall leave the quiet of death in your wake. You will be Jain Zar.'

The Storm of Silence. The first pupil.

21

The beast summoned by the mass sacrifice of the cultists towered above its subjects, who threw themselves onto their faces to make obeisance at its passing. Of the Dark Lady's mortal body, nothing remained. Her new form was black as coal, eyes like sapphires, wings of shadow stretching broad from her back. She advanced on cloven feet, one hand wreathed in a ball of lightning, the other clutching the hilt of a long golden scimitar.

The dark princess stopped some distance from the *Patient Lightning*, sword pointing up to the starry night. The air churned around the blade. A whirl of warp power grew in strength, summoning unnatural black clouds from out of nowhere.

At the daemon princess's feet the cultists gathered, clutching their weapons to their chests, eyes wide with awe and fear at the storm gathering above. Purple energy flickered across the clouds, bathing the battlefield with stark flashes of light. The growl of tank engines was like thunder, rolling across the corpse-littered hillsides.

Confronted by the daemonic storm the aircraft of the eldar dared not approach. Grav-tanks glided into position, their starcannons and brightlances levelled at the monstrosity that confronted them. Aspect Warriors disembarked from their Wave Serpents, taking up positions guarding the approaches to the downed starship, forming knots of colour against the scorched earth.

At a signal from Hylandris, the host opened fire, bright beams of energy and blasts of plasma obliterating the darkness in a flickering display of destruction. A dozen of the humans' tanks exploded and swathes of their infantry fell in moments. Pulses of blue and white converged on the daemon, but the concentrated discharges of energy flared ineffectually from her ebon body.

The daemon lowered her sword, the tip bursting into flame as it pointed towards the *Patient Lightning*. She snarled something in a bestial tongue and the cultists surged forward, a living wave even more desperate and wild than the previous assaults. Drivers gunned the engines of the vehicles and accelerated, their mad charges crushing comrades beneath their tracks. Led by their living god, the Chaos worshippers hurled themselves into the teeth of the eldar defence, dying with smiles and laughter, every death greeted with joy rather than fear.

On board the starship, Hylandris searched for the pilot, Neridiath. She was not where he had left her, so he followed a trail of dismembered and decapitated human bodies until he found her with Asurmen in one of the empty lockers on a lower deck. The corridor outside was choked with corpses, their throats slashed, disembowelled, limbs cut clean away. Axes, knives and guns lay scattered amongst the dead.

Fighting back a wave of nausea, the seer exerted his will and a pulse of psychic energy parted a path through the carcasses, throwing bodies aside in a bloody wave as he strode through the gore. Hylandris stopped at the door to the storage bay, shocked by what he saw.

The Phoenix Lord looked as though he had bathed in blood, the crest of his helm matted with gore, the gonfalon that flew from his back soaked crimson. There were spatters of the same on the face of Neridiath and the child she clutched in her arms as she sat with her back against the wall. Her eyes were locked on Asurmen, or more particularly the shimmering blade in his hand. The floor was slick with a covering of fresh blood that rippled as Asurmen turned.

There was no reaction from Neridiath but the girl in her tight embrace looked at the farseer with innocent eyes.

Afraid. Help?

'The time has come,' Hylandris said, ignoring the child's worried question. 'We can delay no longer, we must take off. Our foe has ascended into the darkness, now a daemon of the warp.'

Asurmen looked at him and the air burned with the aftermath of his rage. Slowly the anger receded into the shell of the Phoenix Lord's armour. He lowered his blade and glanced at the pilot.

'I know,' Asurmen said. He pointed at Neridiath. 'Wake her.'

Hylandris looked at the pilot. She had not moved, sitting staring at some distant scene that existed only in her mind.

'Come back to me,' he said quietly, but there was no reply. Her spirit had sunk within itself, hiding from whatever horror she had witnessed. There was only one way to reach her. Hylandris crouched beside the inert pilot and laid a hand on the child's head.

'I'm sorry,' he said, releasing just an iota of his psychic energy into Manyia.

The child screamed as if stuck with a pin, her psychic cry even more piercing.

PAIN!

An instant later, Hylandris was flat on his back, Neridiath on top of him with a knee on his chest, one hand around the bawling child, the other at his throat, a human dagger in her grasp. Asurmen made no move to defend the farseer.

'Touch my daughter again and I'll kill you,' she snarled. Asurmen suppressed a smile. Events were eventually turning towards the fate he had seen in the vision.

'The ship,' the farseer gasped. 'We are in immense danger. You have to pilot the ship.'

Neridiath stepped back, confused and distant as though waking from a dream. She saw the knife in her hands.

'Did I...?' She shook her head, remembering. Her gaze turned to the Phoenix Lord. 'Asurmen. You slaughtered them all.'

'You would be dead if he had not,' said Hylandris, offering his hand. 'Come, we must leave now or we shall all be dead.'

'The ship... Yes, I was moving to the control chamber, to take the ship away from the attack. But can't you feel it? The distress?'

Asurmen allowed his consciousness to mingle with the essence of the battleship for a moment. He felt the presence of Hylandris close at hand as the farseer psychically interrogated the half-aware spirits that flowed through the matrix.

'The storm, it is sorcerous in nature and could bring us down if it continues to grow,' the farseer announced. 'Even if we drive back the artillery and tanks, the daemon is feeding on the death of its worshippers, drawing strength from their continuing sacrifices.'

Asurmen moved away. 'Get to the control chamber.'

'You can't leave like this,' Hylandris said as the Phoenix Lord stepped out into the passageway. 'Where are you going?'

Asurmen stopped but did not look back. His diresword flared and the blood streamed into the air, leaving the blade glimmering like a sliver of molten gold.

'To fight your daemon.'

'We cannot wait for you.'

'You won't have to.'

22

Most of the humans had been expelled from the ship. Those that remained were herded into killing crossfires by the crew of the *Patient Lightning* and the Guardians of Anuiven that had been lured to Hylandris's cause.

The Aspect Warriors withdrew from the fight, following their exarchs into the lower reaches of the ship. In turn, the exarchs were responding to a call, a psychic beacon that flared in their blood and roused their warrior spirits.

Asurmen waited for them in a broad and high chamber. Once a dock for anti-grav tanks, its contents now lay wrecked and burning on the battlefield surrounding the warship. By shrine-squad and Aspect the warriors assembled. Dire Avengers to the fore, Asurmen's own Aspect. Beside them, the Howling Banshees whose teachings descended from the lessons of Jain Zar, and Fire Dragons of Fuegan, the Dark Reapers that clove to the destructive creed of Maugan Ra. At the edge of the mass lurked the Striking Scorpions, swathed by the psychic shadow that followed them. A handful of Swooping Hawks were all that were left of three shrine-squads that had come, having suffered heavily in the storm unleashed by the Dark Lady. There were others Aspects too. Shining Spears and Warp Spiders, Crimson Hunters and Ebon Talons, whose creators had never been Asurya but whose legacies still echoed through the ages. Those squads whose exarchs had fallen drifted in last, slightly confused, only realising on entering the nature of the urge that had brought them.

'Blood Runs. Anger Rises. Death Wakes. War Calls.' Asurmen's voice stretched easily to the furthest part of the chamber, filling it with his words. The mantra caused all that heard it to stiffen, to stand prouder, their senses and minds fired. 'Battle rages and we must fight its last actions. You leave behind your shrines. I am the only shrine you need. I am Khaine the Avenger, the Hand of Asuryan that strikes down the wicked. Where I stand, you will stand. Where I lead, you will follow. Where I fall, you will avenge.'

He could feel their minds conjoining, their war masks returning with greater vigour, pushing aside all remorse, all mercy, all frailty. These were his warriors, all of them, no matter the Aspect or shrine. The Path was his creation, the war mask his discovery. The senses of all present were attuned to his every word and movement.

'We are Khaine Incarnate. Not the Avatar, a broken shard of violence and death. We, the Aspect Warriors, united. There is no foe we cannot defeat, no enemy we cannot slay, no battle we cannot win when we stand together. As one, as Khaine, we shall destroy the host that besets us, and again prove that the eldar do not relinquish their lives lightly.'

The time had come to rectify his failings on the Jhitaar core world. He was the knot upon the skein, the force that had brought all of these warriors to this place at this time. He forged his own path across the skein, parting the threads of mortals and gathering them when needed. The exarchs had not known why they answered the request of Hylandris, only that they should. The Guardians, the warlocks, the corsairs, all had been unknowing instruments of Asurmen, falling into the wake of his fate like moons trapped in orbit around the gravity well of a world.

That fate had delivered them to Asurmen when he needed them most, just as it had delivered him to them.

As Asurmen strode towards the immense portal where Falcons and Wave Serpents had once disembarked, the shrine-squads parted like a bow wave, a rainbow of colour spreading and then falling into place behind him. He connected his mind to the matrix of the *Patient Lightning,* using it to amplify his thoughts, to send his battle cry into the minds of all the eldar. He needed no shout, no verbal declaration of intent. His will hammered into the minds of all that were part of the matrix, instilling discipline, courage and dedication, a call to war louder and more compelling than any oratory.

He descended the ramp as the gun turrets of the battleship opened fire, a deadly salute to the emerging Phoenix Lord and his warriors. The Shining Spears flitted past, joining Vypers and other jetbike riders to form the point of the descending spear. The air hummed with the crackle of warp jump generators as Warp Spiders slipped across the skein.

Given one will by Asurmen, a single purpose forged

by his strength, the host of the *Patient Lightning* surged from the battleship's bays and boarding bridges, laser and shurikens and plasma heralding the counter-attack.

Crimson hunters launched their aircraft into the ravening storm above, defying the wrath of the Dark Lady to strafe tanks columns and artillery batteries converging on the crashed starship. The last of the Swooping Hawks disappeared towards the cloud, ready to rain las-fire and plasma grenades. Striking Scorpions disappeared into the shadows and Howling Banshees sped ahead on swift feet. With a single purpose, a single fate, the Aspect Warriors attacked.

Asurmen strode into the fray as gunfire lit the sky above and shells tore the ground around him. The Dark Lady's most blessed followers now came forward, those who had stayed close to her and avoided the ambush, determined to prove their worth.

Fusion guns and plasma grenades, shuriken catapults and whirring chainblades greeted the oncoming horde. No robe-clad peasants but armoured warriors with scars and tattoos marking their dedications to the dark powers. Warbands of Chaos, no less, led by Champions and chosen warriors, forged into an army by the will and promises of the Dark Lady.

Asurmen singled out an immense warrior clad in red-and-black war-plate, a banner marked with the rune of the Lord of Skulls flying from a pole upon his back. The Champion of the Blood God charged headlong towards the Dire Avengers that had formed guard around the Phoenix Lord. He held a plasma pistol and immense chain axe, the former forgotten as he unleashed his wrath with the latter. Spittle flew from a fanged mouth, doubtless chanting mindless dedications to his blood-thirsty master.

His armour was riven with hundreds of shurikens, his flesh tattered and bloody in moments, but the Champion paid no heed to the fusillades of the Dire Avengers, laughing as blood coursed down his face and exposed arms. Asurmen moved quickly, sprinting to the fore of his followers. His blade met the oncoming Champion as a silver flash, the tip sliding through the monstrous human's throat.

Asurmen did not even break stride as he left his Aspect Warriors to deal with the Khornate lord's retinue. His gaze was set on the Dark Lady, a towering black presence beyond a sea of foes. Another howling beast of a Champion threw himself at Asurmen and a moment later the warlord's head was spinning to the ground.

The Aspect Warriors advanced in the wake of the Phoenix Lord, a splash of colour across the dark, bloodied turf. As Asurmen slashed and dismembered all that came upon him, so the blade of Khaine cleaved into the army of the Dark Lady, aimed for the daemonic presence at its heart.

23

Pain throbbed up Nymuyrisan's spine, mirroring the damage to the wraithknight. It felt as though he could not move, but it was just fear that kept him frozen. The Chaos beast-machine moved away, lumbering towards the battleship, the handlers believing the wraithknight destroyed. Nymuyrisan considered the possibility that they were not that wrong. There was no response from Jarithuran and the wraithknight's systems, but for life support and basic sensory input, which were malfunctioning.

Nymuyrisan realised that it was not only the Chaos followers that perhaps thought the wraithknight dead. The other eldar were retreating, moving back onto the battleship with the humans in pursuit. He also realised he did not care. The emptiness, the loneliness had returned with the second loss of Jarithuran. Better to die here than to continue in a meaningless existence without his twin.

As his thoughts turned to the morbid, he detected a

trickle of activity in the wraithknight's core structure. It was barely a glimmer, but he focused on it, nurturing it with his thoughts as one might try to fan a newborn flame. He disabled the barriers that kept his mind from being wholly integrated into the wraithknight, erasing safeguards that stopped him from experiencing full interaction with the wraithbone core.

Immediately the pain went from a dull throb to a piercing agony, his chest feeling as though the ribs on the right side were splayed open.

Nymuyrisan passed out.

When he awoke, the pain had subsided slightly. The wraithknight's limbs twitched as Nymuyrisan's awakened brain impulses flooded into its control circuit.

Data was still coming in across the communications network and Nymuyrisan took a moment to analyse what was happening. Many of the humans had been drawn onto the battleship and destroyed, and Asurmen led the counter-attack.

The Phoenix Lord spearheaded the thrust towards the daemon summoned by the Chaos worshippers, striding through the las-fire and shells slaying all that he met. Nymuyrisan watched with amazement as the Phoenix Lord was engulfed by a detonation, disappearing from view for a moment as flame and smoke billowed. He reappeared, none the worse for the experience, pouring a storm of shuriken-fire into the foe.

Where Asurmen fought, the eldar drove back the infantry and tanks in range of the *Patient Lightning*. To be on the same battlefield as the legendary warrior filled Nymuyrisan with a mixture of emotions. Pride was tempered by foreboding. The Phoenix Lords were semi-mythical, appearing at pivotal moments in a craftworld's history. Did the arrival of Asurmen signal the salvation of Anuiven or its doom? Whatever the outcome, Nymuyrisan and the others had become part of the ongoing legend.

Though his senses were dulled Nymuyrisan could feel energy starting to grow inside the frame of the battleship. The spirit circuit of the wraithknight resonated with the increased activity of the ship's matrix as *Patient Lightning*'s psychic heart grew in strength.

The ship was readying to take off.

There was a problem, obvious to the wraithknight pilot. The moment the eldar withdrew to their ship the humans would be after them, able to batter the ascending starship with cannons and lasers. In order to save the ship, the army would have to stay on the ground.

Nymuyrisan discovered that he could not disconnect from the datastream. He was not simply accessing the wraithknight's systems, his psychic potential was powering them. Its sensors were his senses. Even more than before, he had become part of the machine. If he concentrated he could feel his heart beating, but only in as much that he detected its vibrations inside the organic component located in his chest cavity. His consciousness was no longer contained inside his flesh, but encompassed by the embodiment of the wraithknight. His mortal shell had been reduced to the status of power source, nothing more than a battery of psychic and biological energy to draw upon.

'Hello.'

Such a mundane word, but filled with such portent and emotion. Nymuyrisan's mood soared as he recognised the voice of his brother, unheard for so long.

'Hello,' he replied, unable to think of anything else to say.

He could feel Jarithuran, the twin spirits occupying the same body, which was a reverse, because for all of their mortal existence it had felt as if they had been one spirit split between two forms.

Now they were closer than they could ever have been in mortal life. They shared not only circuit, limbs and body but also the integral material of the circuit, the same meta-existence as each other. It was as though Nymuyrisan looked at his reflection, but from behind the mirror.

He wondered for a moment if Jarithuran was really still with him. The sensation was so strange it could have been a trick of the mind caused by the systems of the wraithknight.

'I am here,' said Jarithuran. 'Truly. We are the same but independent.'

'I am sorry I got you killed, Jarith.' The twin's sorrow was his brother's sorrow too, but it was returned as sorrow for Nymuyrisan's guilt.

'I forgive you,' said Jarithuran.

Though he had felt his brother's compassion and acceptance countless times, it made all the difference to hear the words – at least to have the sentiment framed in words. It made them real in a way that any amount of sympathetic feeling could not.

'We seem to be in trouble,' Nymuyrisan said, focusing on their current predicament. 'I think we will be abandoned.'

'It does not matter, we cannot survive long. Without your will to sustain it, your body will quickly wither, and without the biological seat of your psyche to power us these thoughts will soon disappear.'

'How long?'

'How would I know, I've been a wraithknight no longer than you!'

'You've been dead far longer...'

Jarithuran had no answer to that. Instead the twin encouraged his brother to match his thought-impulses, opening the fingers of the right hand. Between them they carried enough psychic-signal to activate the nerve-bundles and pseudomuscles of their war engine. Cautiously, they moved the right arm and hand until the splayed fingers fell upon the haft of the dropped ghostglaive. Closing their fingers around the weapon, Nymuyrisan and Jarithuran shared a moment of accomplishment, both of them mentally smiling at each other.

'We can still fight,' they thought in unison.

'The more we do, the quicker we shall burn up what's left of your body,' Jarithuran warned. 'We will not have very long at all, I fear.'

'It is of no consequence. I have already been granted a wish beyond consideration – to share even another heartbeat with you is a gift that is priceless. Better to end in swift glory, as we should have done, than to eke out our last efforts to prolong our reunion.'

Conjoined in thought and intent, the two brothers lifted the wraithknight to one knee and then stood up. The left arm was gone, the same side of the chestplate irrevocably broken, exposing vital circuitry and Nymuyrisan's mortal body. Hefting the ghostglaive in one hand, they searched the battlefield for the Chaos beast, eager to restore the balance of pride.

The starcannons were still operational and they unleashed a storm of miniature suns as they strode into the Chaos army, the blaze of fire taking the daemon's followers unawares. The ghostglaive slashed through those too slow to get out of the war machine's path or insane enough to hurl themselves at the wraithknight in their battle-frenzy.

'Hylandris, can you hear us?'

There was a moment of distance and emptiness and then the farseer's mind connected to the circuitry of the wraithknight.

Remarkable, possibly foolish. You realise that you will not be able to sustain this state for long?

'Long enough to cover a retreat,' said Jarithuran.

'We will keep the enemy back until you have taken off,' added Nymuyrisan.

It will be done, the farseer promised.

At the moment of disconnection Nymuyrisan found the Chaos beast. Its cannon was pounding the aft section of the battleship, each warpflame-shrouded shell leaving a burned welt on the skin of the *Patient Lightning*, the charring spreading like an infection from each impact spot. It would take only a few more hits until the hull was breached.

The twins broke into a sprint, joyful at a shared memory of the races they used to run around the Dome of Skies on Anuiven. The wraithknight pounded forward at speed, fuelled by their attempts to outpace each other even though they shared the same body, legs moving in a blur.

The eldar were already falling back. Nymuyrisan noticed that the grav-tank crews were exiting their vehicles, leaving them in the charge of the spirits that helped control them. The wraithknight pilots were not the only dead that would sacrifice their immortal futures to protect the living.

The Chaos behemoth saw them coming and turned to face their charge. Splinters of armour flew from the wraithknight's body as secondary cannons and machine guns spewed fire. Now that he was fully part of the construct Nymuyrisan could feel each strike like a tiny bite on his flesh.

'Stop that!' Jarithuran's admonition jarred through Nymuyrisan's thoughts. 'I can feel it too. We're dead, pain is simply an illusion, a memory of what came before. Stop remembering it for me!'

Contrite, Nymuyrisan tried his best not to think of the impacts all over his body as pain. They were... rain. The gentle patter of precipitation, invigorating and delightful.

'Much better,' said Jarithuran.

The behemoth's main cannon roared but the shot went wide, the pair of screaming skull shells flying high past the wraithknight's shoulder.

'Our turn,' the twins thought.

The starcannons raked plasma along the nearest flank of the beast, punching through armoured howdahs and searing into scaled flesh. The behemoth roared in pain, its horned head arching back. Having seen what had become of the other beast, the Chaos followers were abandoning their mount, leaping from their turrets, swinging to the ground on ropes and sliding down ladders. Left to its own instincts, the Chaos beast shucked off the towers and turrets, rearing up to throw the buildings from its back.

It crashed down, newly revealed black hide pocked with old wounds. Some of the armour remained, on the shoulders and spine, melded to the flesh by evil sorcery. Chainmail with links the size of a man's head hung in a mask over its face, swinging and rattling as the behemoth opened its mouth and bellowed a challenge.

It lowered its head and charged at the wraithknight, the ground trembling. Nymuyrisan looked at the approaching beast and realised that there was no fear in him. He had nothing to lose and so the dread of losing everything had disappeared too.

Moving as one, the twins guided the wraithknight aside, three quick strides taking them out of the charging behemoth's path. As it passed, they struck, spinning to slash the ghostglaive across the creature's throat. Nymuyrisan felt an odd moment of contact as the psychically charged blade seared through skin and blood vessels, almost feeling the life spirit of the behemoth coursing through its body.

The sensation passed as the blade tore free from the creature's neck, cleaving through spine and muscle with ease. The beast stumbled and then collapsed, falling to its knees before rolling sideways into the muck.

The moment of victory, the heartbeat between the act and the realisation of what they had done, swelled up between the twins, a shared experience like nothing else Nymuyrisan had encountered. There was no guilt, no consequences to worry about. He was not dying, he was dead, fast becoming a memory of himself. Soon even that would no longer exist.

His awareness of reality was drifting away, draining from his thoughts even as life drained from his body, absorbed by the vampiric need of the wraithknight. By his need. By their need.

The battleship was almost forgotten, names were inconsequential, this battle, this world were old concerns. The past and future were fast becoming irrelevant. He and Jarithuran had become the wraithknight, with one purpose left to fulfil. To slay until slain.

Turning towards the remaining humans, the wraithknight raised the ghostglaive high, blood streaming down the energised blade.

Life had ended. All that remained was death. Release. Nymuyrisan lost the last piece of the tether, the final vestige of himself that separated him from the wraithknight, from his brother.

The twins would not make the final journey alone.

24

In the absence of the retreating eldar, most of the humans fell upon each other to demonstrate their devotion to their newly born goddess. The daemon princess revelled in the internecine fighting, channelling the dissipating hope and aspiration into itself to strengthen the duct between her corporeal form and the warp. Overhead the storm flickered and bellowed, infused by and mirroring the violence unleashed on the ground below.

A few eldar had not been able to make it to the battleship. Knowing that they had been abandoned they did not try to slink away but fought on alongside the spirits of the dead that were guiding the Falcons and Wave Serpents and Vypers. The daemon strode across the battlefield, unleashing bolts of lightning at these survivors as well as her own minions. She cut left and right with the golden blade, hewing limbs and heads from her followers, drinking in the flickers of psychic power released by their deaths. With each slaying, with each draught of life essence, the daemon grew stronger.

Asurmen had chosen to stay. He was needed here, to hold back the threat of the Dark Lady. He had thought his task complete with the delivery of Neridiath to the battleship, but he should have known Asuryan required a far greater deed of him.

The storm was centred on the daemon princess. While she remained intent on the *Patient Lightning* it would be all but impossible for the ship to leave. It was not the first time the Phoenix Lord had confronted a mortal elevated to daemonhood and he knew their weakness. The Dark Lady required warp power to secure the transition from physical human to metaphysical incarnation of Chaos. The link was raw, vulnerable and could be broken if he inflicted enough damage.

The newly raised also shared another weakness: pride. Buoyed up by the answer to their dark prayers, infused with power they had sought for a lifetime, they believed themselves invincible, suddenly beyond mortal concerns. The eldar and the battleship had been a means to an end, the fulcrum on which her bargain for power had been balanced. Even if he could not slay the Dark Lady outright, he could certainly move her attention away from the others and give them time to escape.

He sent a mental command to a nearby Vyper. The large jetbike swooped towards him, the gun cradle on its back empty. Pulling himself up behind the shuriken cannon, Asurmen bid the vehicle take him towards the daemon. As they closed, he unleashed a spray of fire from the shuriken cannon. The hail of projectiles thudded into the daemon's unnatural flesh without any evident effect save for the one Asurmen had intended – to gain the warp-monster's attention.

Seeing the Phoenix Lord the daemon princess uttered a piercing cry and spread her wings. She lifted into the air. The black-skinned creature arrowed towards the circling Vyper. Asurmen ascended too, taking the daemon further and further from the ongoing battle and the waves of death that sustained her. Soon the Vyper reached its maximum height, a skimmer not a true flyer, and its anti-grav engines whined to maintain their altitude. The daemon princess suffered no such limits, quickly closing on the craft from behind.

Thoughts meshed with the dead spirit controlling the Vyper, Asurmen led the Dark Lady on a chase across the forest, firing the shuriken cannon at the daemon whenever he thought she might be losing interest. Snarling, she flew faster and faster, almost catching up with the speeding Vyper, the distance from the battle growing greater with every passing heartbeat.

I shall enjoy devouring your soul when I catch you. The daemon's voice was inside Asurmen's head, a hissing whisper. *You cannot run from me forever.*

'I can,' replied Asurmen, 'but you mistake my intent.'

With a thought he swept the Vyper down to a clearing, leaping from its back as it skimmed just above the ground. Rolling, he came to his feet and turned just as the daemon princess arrived.

The daemon was quick, golden blade snaking out to meet Asurmen's cut towards her throat. The two swords met, exploding with psychic and warp power. Asurmen took a step back, ducking to avoid a barb-edged wing that lashed towards his face.

The daemon turned as she passed, furling her wings to land a distance away. She stood for a moment, watching Asurmen, warp energy cracking from her fist.

What are you? the Dark Lady asked. *I see you properly now, with immortal eyes. Beneath that armour, you are not eldar.*

'I am,' Asurmen replied. 'As much as you are human, at least.'

I have ascended, the daemon boasted, spreading her arms wide. *I am immortal! You cannot compare to my magnificence.*

Asurmen walked slowly towards the daemon princess, his blade at the ready.

'Look at me, what do you see?'

I see... The daemon recoiled in confusion. *I see nothing. You do not exist.*

'You should not cast such aspersions,' said Asurmen. 'You are not exactly here either. A projection, a shadow cast from the warp.'

But you are not a daemon. She flapped her wings in agitation. *I can feel your warp reflection, it is strong. You are there, but you are not here. That is not possible.*

'Where is the human that you were?' said Asurmen, stopping a couple of dozen paces from the daemon. 'Where has she gone?'

She is in me, become me, the daemon replied. *I am her.*

'But you are not. She was human and you are a daemon. You cannot be both. She is dead. You killed her when you ascended.'

I live on, I am not dead. I have become immortal.

'That remains to be tested,' said Asurmen.

He opened fire, scything shurikens across the

daemon's midsection. Enraged more than harmed, the beast replied with a blast of lightning. Asurmen had anticipated the attack and had already moved, swiftly circling to the left, shurikens flying from his vambraces. He cut back to the right and dived as the daemon hurled another bolt of warp power. Closing the gap he dodged left and right, firing alternately with right and left arm, never remaining in one place for more than a heartbeat. The Dark Lady threw another blast of power in frustration, missing once again.

The shurikens had not inflicted much damage but the daemon expended power to maintain its corporeal body and shrug off the slicing rounds. More importantly, the daemon princess was enraged by the incessant hail of shurikens, pride blinding her to any concern other than the destruction of Asurmen.

With a single bound the daemon cleared the intervening distance, swiping her blade towards the Phoenix Lord's chest. The Sword of Asur leapt up to meet the attack with a mind of its own. The spirit stone in its pommel blazed with energy as the two blades collided, erupting with expended power.

Still firing short bursts of shurikens into the daemon, Asurmen ducked under her sword arm, slicing her wing. He ducked as the Dark Lady pivoted, golden blade swinging for his neck. The top of Asurmen's blade flashed as it met daemon flesh, leaving a trail of burning blood dripping from the creature's thigh.

The other wing slashed unexpectedly at the Phoenix Lord, a clawed joint catching him on the shoulder. The blow sent him spinning to the ground. Snarling in triumph the daemon lunged, but Asurmen rolled aside a moment before the golden daemonblade hit, avoiding the weapon as it speared into the ground beside him. He aimed a burst of shurikens into the daemon's face and sprang to his feet as she reared back, stung by the attack.

For a third time golden blade and diresword met, the furious detonation of their contact almost knocking Asurmen from his feet. The daemon princess was new-born and naive, but swollen on recently released warp power. She was expending that energy at a prodigious rate, siphoning more and more power from the warp to fuel her presence in the material realm.

A bolt of lightning spewed from the daemon's eyes, striking Asurmen in the chest in a fountain of black motes. Hurled backwards, Asurmen twisted to turn the fall into a roll. He swerved to the left as he regained his feet, back towards the daemon, but another bolt of power caught him, slamming into his lower spine. Armour split as he was propelled face first into the ground.

Your arrogance has betrayed you, the daemon said as Asurmen rolled onto his back. She paced forward, crackling energy wreathed about her raised fist.

'Do you really think this is the time to gloat?' Asurmen fired both vambraces at once, a slew of shurikens slashing into the daemon's chest. She staggered, giving him time to jump to his feet, and just enough time to raise his sword to parry the golden blade that swiftly descended towards his head. The shock of the impact knocked him down to one knee but the Phoenix Lord held firm, turning aside the next blow with the flat of his diresword.

Your weapons cannot hurt me, the daemon princess insisted, smashing her scimitar into the Phoenix Lord's blade, forcing him back.

Asurmen countered as the daemon advanced, suddenly launching himself at the creature. He was inside her reach in a moment, driving his blade point-first into her chest. Psychic power surged from the spirit stone, pulsing fire into the wound.

Screaming, the daemon reeled back, flailing away from the Phoenix Lord as white flame burst out of the wound in her chest. Shrieking, the daemon tumbled down, wings furling about her.

Asurmen retreated a few steps, sword held level to guard his withdrawal. The kneeling daemon twitched, shoulders moving up and down with what looked like sobbing. Asurmen launched himself at the monster, leaping high, blade pointed down to drive between the shoulder blades.

The daemon princess whipped around as he left the ground. The daemon's parody of a face grinned, revealing a row of needle fangs. The tip of her scimitar swept up towards the descending Phoenix Lord.

There was nothing he could do as the immense golden blade crashed against his chest, splitting armour from ribs to shoulder. The force of the blow threw him across the clearing, spinning and rolling, to crash into the ground almost at the treeline.

Now your soul will be mine! The daemon advanced again, steaming blood pouring from the puncture in her chest.

Asurmen struggled to his feet, sword held up in defiance.

Even your magic blade cannot kill me. The daemon pulled back her sword arm, ready for the final blow.

'We shall see,' said Asurmen. He looked up. 'I have other weapons.'

Hull glowing red from the heat of re-entry, *Stormlance* blazed across the forest, setting the trees on fire with its passing. Pulsars stabbed out beams of raw power, striking the daemon princess square in the chest. The laser blasts seared straight through the daemon, leaving neat round holes. The daemon looked down in disbelief and then back up at the warship screaming overhead. She swayed slightly and returned her gaze to the Phoenix Lord. As she turned she opened her mouth, no doubt to utter some further taunt about the ineffectiveness of Asurmen's weapons.

Taking advantage of the momentary distraction by *Stormlance*, the Phoenix Lord leapt, sword lancing out in front of him. The tip punched into the mouth of the daemon and out through the back of her head, fire licking along the blade. The Phoenix Lord's knee smashed into the Dark Lady's wounded chest and he rode the falling daemon's body to the ground, while white flame engulfed her head.

Throwing himself clear, the Phoenix Lord rolled to his feet and turned in time to see the last of the creature's form consumed by the cleansing fire. Not for the Dark Lady banishment to the warp. Her immortality had been fake, a lie, false hope to trap the greedy and vain. Daemons could certainly die, their essence dissipated forever by certain artefacts or conjurations. The Sword of Asur was one such treasure.

Did we win? asked *Stormlance* as the craft circled overhead, bleeding off speed.

'Not yet.' Asurmen gazed towards the heavens. 'The battle was never going to be decided here.'

25

Neridiath followed Hylandris into the main control chamber of the *Patient Lightning*. She had expected something grandiose, far larger than the control pod of the *Joyous Venture,* but found herself in a chamber about twice as big as the one on the tradeship. The main difference was the number of stations at each function. Two eldar sat at the sensor banks and four manned the weapons arrays. There were three empty cradles at the pilots' position and Neridiath turned a questioning look to the farseer.

'It is good practice for a ship of this complexity to be steered by three pilots,' he told her, 'but it is not essential. Think of it as a redundancy. Quickly, the enemy attack cannot be stalled for long, we must reach sufficient altitude to avoid their resurgent ire.'

'We cannot fly blindly into the void,' said Neridiath, taking a walk around the control chamber, using the moment to familiarise herself, seeking to calm herself after the dash to the control pod. She needed her own equilibrium if she was going to guide the starship to safety. She introduced herself to the two crew manning the scanning stations.

'I am Lymandris,' replied the first, and waved a hand to her partner, who bowed his head in brief acknowledgement. 'This is Kazaril.'

'How much function do the scanners have?'

'We have redirected the bulk of the scanning arrays to forward, leaving us blind to aft,' said Kazaril.

'I've got no plans to look back, anyway,' said Lymandris as she approached the piloting suite.

'Very well, as long as we can see it, I'll try not to crash into it,' said Neridiath. It was her plan to run and run fast, whatever Asurmen had said about the need for battle. The lustre of excitement had worn off this escapade the moment the daemons had taken her friends and all she wanted now was to be far away from danger and the temptation of battle.

She ignored the gunners, telling herself they would not be needed, and stopped behind the nearest piloting cradle. She hesitated for a moment, looking down at Manyia. The child was exhausted from her travails and slept restlessly. Placing a kiss on her forehead, Neridiath handed her daughter to Hylandris. 'She trusts you, for some reason I don't know. Please, make her dreams less fraught.'

'I will,' said the farseer, surprised. He took Manyia and folded over the voluminous sleeve of his robe like a blanket.

Emptying her thoughts of everything else, Neridiath slipped into the cradle, letting it engulf her with its psycho-reactive mesh; at once she felt the familiar sensation of being cocooned. Instinctively she set her thoughts free, finding a foundation in the ship's matrix.

The first thing the pilot felt was the residual taint of the humans. There were a few still alive aboard the ship, most of them wounded, the others being hunted down. Outside the storm raged, lashing the hull with tendrils of warp power. Each bolt was like the unwelcome touch of a stranger, making Neridiath's skin crawl.

Something even worse drifted into her thoughts. Flashes of fire, of the air screaming past, of mayhem and pain. The starship was crashing, the flare of its atmospheric entry coursing through its systems.

There was a moment of blankness and Neridiath recoiled, her thoughts crumbling under the numbness of the comatose pilots that had last interacted with the navigational systems. It was a heart-wrenching sensation, as if the universe had opened up and swallowed their minds whole. Steeling her thoughts against the horror of their after-image, Neridiath pushed aside the memory remnants, clearing the pilot suite of all distraction, leaving just the purity of the psychic matrix.

A tremble ran through her body and was copied by the ship as the gravity drive awakened at her insistence. Neridiath could feel the repairs made by Basir Runemaster, fresh wounds scabbed over, the matrix and the engines still raw in places. The *Patient Lightning* was hesitant, wary of these injuries, but Neridiath pushed on, exerting her will over the incorporeal spirits that powered and partly controlled the ship.

With a lurch the battleship lifted from the ground, a moment of disorientation while the inertia dampeners adjusted for operation within a gravity field. It was not only the systems that were careful, it had been a long time since Neridiath had manoeuvred from an actual planet – most of her voyages had begun and ended in the void of outer space.

The gravity drive was labouring slightly, stuttering and surging in the tempest, but she rode with it, easing out the jerks with small adjustments to trim and lift. The ship responded, the mesh between pilot and vessel deepening as both became more familiar with each other.

The storm suddenly abated, the crushing presence of the warp dissipating around the *Patient Lightning*. Neridiath felt a pulse of happiness running through the matrix, from both the living and the dead.

Gathering confidence and momentum, pilot and battleship lifted together, riding the buffeting of crosswinds that strengthened as the starship's altitude increased. A brief foray into the sensor suite revealed the land dropping away with increasing rapidity, the humans soon reduced to specks and then a dark smudge pouring through the forest. A few heartbeats later and the forest was lost as the *Patient Lightning* reached the cloud layer, still accelerating.

The atmosphere thinned, the boundary between air and space a vague greyness. Neridiath fought the urge to hold her breath as the air pressure dropped and dropped until there was nothing left. She could sense the pull of the world's gravity well decreasing too. The grav-engines were operating more smoothly, coasting the battleship away from the planet.

A sense of freedom swept through Neridiath, the spray of stars laid out before her, open void beckoning.

Her thoughts were interrupted by an urgent imposition

from Kazaril at the sensor panel. Three jagged shapes were in motion, heading straight towards them, energy surging to their strange weapons.

The battleship's instinct was to turn and fight. Neridiath fought the urge, instructing the *Patient Lightning* to direct more power to the engines. There was resistance, costing valuable time, but eventually the pilot enforced her will on the vessel, demanding all available power be directed to the engines.

Another skim through the sensor banks confirmed what she feared. The Chaos vessels were picking up speed far more swiftly than any normal human vessel. At full capacity the *Patient Lightning* would easily outrun them, but the battleship was far from operating at its maximum potential.

'Madam pilot, we must reduce speed and manoeuvre for combat,' one of the gunners interjected into her thoughts. 'At current trajectories, we will be vulnerable to enemy fire before we have reached a safe distance. We will be unable to defend ourselves if we simply try to flee.

'We must attack.'

The *Patient Lightning* sped away from Escatharinesh on a surge of gravitic energy leaving a silvery wake of energised particles glinting in the starlight. Neridiath commanded the battleship to unfurl its solar sails, trying to glean every last ounce of power she could. The fresh energy input increased their speed a little, but the reports from Kazaril were not encouraging. Two of the three enemy ships would most likely pass within range of the battleship.

'We must slow to combat speed and divert power to the holofields as well as the weapons batteries,' Kazaril insisted, the call echoed by others on the control deck.

'How much more power do we need to get clear?' Neridiath asked in reply. 'How much more speed can we get?'

There was a pause while Kazaril consulted the matrix. He spoke without conviction.

'Perhaps another five per cent? Assuming the gravity drive can cope with that much power.'

'What if I reduce the environment systems? We can fly in the dark.'

'Two per cent gain, at most,' Kazaril told her. 'And that would be reducing atmospheric processing to a minimum as well.'

'What if we drop scanning and all weapons control?'

'What if you just do as we say and reduce speed ready for battle?' snapped one of the gunners. 'We are wasting time. It does not matter how much more energy you squeeze out of the gravity engines, we are not going to get away. We must be prepared. We have no idea what sort of weapons those vessels possess. One hit may cripple us. We have to go on the offensive!'

'Incoming signal for you,' said Kazaril before Neridiath could reply. He pushed across a sliver of the sensory banks into Neridiath's consciousness.

A speck of power was bursting out of the upper atmosphere of Escatharinesh, an arrowhead of white light and fire. Neridiath recognised it immediately, her shock blurted out in a mental impulse.

Stormlance!

XII

After getting Jain Zar to retrace her steps, it did not take long to find the small ship that had brought the cultists back from the webway. Asurmen recognised it as an old class of pleasure yacht, once used for corona-skimming in stars and satellite cruises. The blood-drinkers had added two crude weapon pods to the sides, sporting long-barrelled cannons.

'Can you fly one of these?' asked Jain Zar.

'Simple enough,' he replied. 'It should have a mental command circuit.'

The door hissed open at their approach, descending to form a boarding ramp. The ship itself was not very big, intended for no more than twenty passengers. The interior was a mess, the floor stained with drag marks of blood, most of the cabins equally soiled. Asurmen found a chamber near the stern that was not too badly despoiled and deposited his bag on the bed with a clink of crystals.

'What are those?' asked Jain Zar, pointing at the coloured gems as they slipped onto the fraying sheet.

'I call them affinity stones,' said Asurmen. 'They form a psychic bond with you. When you die, they capture your spirit. You should have one.'

He picked up a stone and tossed it to Jain Zar. It flickered into life as she caught it, glittering with white light.

'Why would I want one?' she replied, looking uncertainly at the gem, caressing it with a fingertip. 'Why do I want my spirit trapped in one of these things for eternity?'

'Because I think the alternative is much, much worse. Trust me.'

She accepted this with a nod and followed him back to the control deck. The bridge was relatively clean and clear of grisly decoration, and the panels lit up as they entered. Asurmen located the pilot's couch and sat down, gesturing for Jain Zar to sit next to him.

'I should be able to tell the ship where we want to go and it will do the rest,' he said. This impulse of desire was enough to start the ship. It silently ascended, closing the hatchway as it lifted over the city.

From this viewpoint the scale of the catastrophe was stark. Daemonic spires sprawled where habitation towers had once stood, like hives of malign beasts with impossibly angled walkways and doors, whose presence contorted the dimensions of space around them. Fires of bright purple and green burned from pyres of eldar corpses, the spirit flames shaped into weeping, wailing faces. Clawed monstrosities capered and danced around the fires, laughing and singing.

As they continued to rise, the details faded, leaving only a scene of total destruction. Towers had toppled, bridges and aerial rails fallen, canals and rivers turned to black sludge that had burst the banks. Asurmen saw the arena *park, now a wild forest of fanged and thorny vegetation that thrashed with manic sentience.*

The arena itself was choked with people, the dead left in place by the whim of their newly birthed god, in the seats where they had bayed and cried for blood with such determination that they ignored the fall of the world around them. Asurmen imagined the gamblers outside had continued to make their wagers until the very moment that their essence was stolen.

Higher still and all that remained was a glistening whiteness. The glow of affinity stones covered the city, each one marking a dead eldar. In the city centre the streets were ablaze, and in dense patches further out where the desperate eldar had come together in their panic and grief. Elsewhere the stones were sparser, until their glow was lost with distance.

'They look like tears,' said Jain Zar, turning her affinity stone over in her hands. 'The tears of a goddess, perhaps, weeping for all the dead.'

'A last gift to us from Isha, maybe?' suggested Asurmen.

'From who? Isha?'

'Isha was a goddess. The first, mother of all the eldar...'
Asurmen began.

26

Asurmen raced after the battleship, his own ship's golden sails gleaming. *Stormlance* extended its matrix, locking with the psychic circuitry of the *Patient Lightning*. Amongst the hundreds of spirits on board, the ship located Neridiath and made contact with the pilot.

Isn't this spectacular? There was a vicious rasp to the warship's thoughts, its enthusiasm for the coming battle lapping at Neridiath's mind like waves slowly eroding a cliff.

The Phoenix Lord realised what *Stormlance* was trying to do – break through the dam of resistance Neridiath had erected with her fear of violence. Asurmen's bloodlust, the part of his spirit that powered the warship, was trying to rip aside her defences to expose the hate and anger being so ruthlessly suppressed. That energy had to be released carefully, in controlled fashion, not unleashed like a beast slipped from a chain.

Can you not feel– The starship's message ended

abruptly when Asurmen took control, forcing aside the lesser part of his spirit.

Listen carefully, Neridiath. This is the moment foreseen, the time that Asuryan dreamed of so long ago. Our fates stand upon the edge of a blade and the choice is yours.

'You cannot force me to kill. And do not try to appeal to my sense of duty with speeches about the future of our people. There are always alternatives.'

Not always. Asurmen accompanied his words with a blunt thrust of psychic power, like a mental slap. *Millions will die because of your misguided principles.*

'Are you going to tell me that killing can serve a higher cause?' Neridiath was trying to withdraw, pulling her mind away from his, humiliated by his insistence. Her reply was carried on a barb of spite. 'Is that your philosophy, to remove the anger and the hate so that killing is just a casual act, devoid of feeling? I will not share your filthy desire for bloodshed!'

Nothing could be further from my philosophy, petulant child! Again the Phoenix Lord allowed his emotion to seep into the contact, a wave of crushing disdain. Neridiath was resisting for the sake of resistance, her contrary personality forcing her to take opposition against all good reason. She tried to ignore him, but he would not let her. The time for subtle cajoling was over. More direct coercion was required.

There is nothing noble about death or killing. The need to fight, the desire to kill, comes only from the worst of our emotions. Jealousy, hatred, anger, revenge, greed. And fear. Your fear. My lesson is not to turn away from these desires, these base instincts that are part of what we are. We must embrace them and channel them, lest they consume us and all around. You will not fight to save our people, but you must *fight to save yourself.*

'Was it easy?' she snapped, letting her frustration slash along the psychic link. It tumbled ineffectively from the iron mind of the Phoenix Lord. 'The first one you killed? Did it give you the thirst for more? I would rather the galaxy was swallowed whole than set foot along that path to destruction.'

You want to know about the first life I took? A freezing chill swept from Asurmen into Neridiath, the cool wrath of the Phoenix Lord manifesting in her body. *I will show you.*

XIII

Illiathin followed closely behind Tethesis, with Maesin just a few steps behind. The three of them stopped as they reached the edge of what had once been the Plaza of Tangential Ascendance. The skybridge that had once arced high over the city had fallen, a broken span wreathed with strange pink growths like vines coiled about a tree trunk. The collapse of the bridge had showered stone on the surrounding district and dammed the river, so that there was ankle-deep purplish water lapping at their feet as they cautiously entered the plaza.

The jagged remains of an auditorium stood out in silhouette against the strange light that came from the black sun, its upper floors shattered in such a way that it resembled a slender skull. A few of the banners that had lined the roof wafted gently despite the lack of wind, giving the impression of tufts of hair.

Illiathin shuddered and looked away, the sensation of being watched ever-present. If the mood of the city had been oppressive before the cataclysm, the atmosphere had become cloying and claustrophobic. The air was sluggish in his lungs, the sound of water against the buildings melancholy.

'Over here,' said Maesin, pointing to the tumbled remains to the left. The building had been an artistic commune once, though the art on display had become bizarre, grotesque, even as the moral malaise of the pre-cataclysm had grown. Some of the works remained outside – sculptures made from animated flesh melded with stone, psychoplastic and metal, and paintings of nightmarish scenes of torture and violence splashed in disturbingly trite pastel colours that masked the depravity that was illustrated.

Maesin took the lead up the steps, a carbine ready in her hands. Tethesis was similarly armed, as was Illiathin, though the weapon felt awkward in his grasp. He had managed to survive the catastrophe without resorting to violence and he had no intention of changing that habit. If there was any threat, he would run. He had warned the others of this, to expect no heroics on his part.

They each readied their activated gleamgems, bathing the interior of the building with beams of bluish light. The lower floor was one large open space, a triangle of three columns forming the central structure of the tower. A moving staircase was still working, its motor purring gently in the stillness. Half-completed pieces, piles of materials and digital easels were arranged across the space. There were bodies strewn on the laminated floor, some still holding their brushes, sculpting tools and rendering wands. Illiathin counted seven in all. A bloody mess at the bottom of a staircase made eight, but he was not sure.

They picked through the debris, lured by Maesin's prom-
ise that she had seen a cache of working power cells on her
previous foraging expedition. Illiathin was careful where
he put his feet, aware of the fluids that lay in puddles, con-
vinced many of them were not simply artistic in origin.

They had made it to the ascending stepway at the back
of the building when a sound caused them all to stop and
turn. It had sounded like a drip of liquid, a splash in a
puddle. The light of the gleamgems roved back and forth
but revealed nothing. Illiathin waited and watched while
the other two turned back to the stairway. He was sure
he heard scraping.

Something moved, a darkness against the ruddy twi-
light that seeped through the open door. Illiathin grabbed
his gleamgem and swung the light across the room. The
beam settled on the staring, slack-jawed face of an eldar.
The body was crawling towards them, dragging itself with
twitching hands. There was something wrong, other than
the obvious. Two horns jutted from its brow, growing in
length as he watched.

He hissed a warning to the others, transfixed by the
apparition. It was changing, growing in some fashion.
The pale, flaccid skin tightened, bones rearranged, the
nose melting away to reveal flared nostrils, the eyes com-
ing to life with a silver glow. It rose to a crawl and then
into a crouch, the fingers of its hands melding, extending,
becoming the tines of long claws.

'Daemon!' yelled Maesin, opening fire with her carbine.
The pulse of red energy slammed into the creature, throw-
ing it back across the room, a gaping hole in its chest.

The daemon slid to a halt at the base of one of the pil-
lars, neck kinked at a strange angle. With a tearing wet

sound, the corpse's skin split. Like an obscene butterfly emerging from its cocoon, the daemon pulled itself free of the body, organs draped from its shoulders in viscous ribbons.

'There's another!' yelped Illiathin, swinging his gleamgem to the left. In the sudden light, the daemon-possessed corpse stumbled, one hand held up to ward away the glare.

Maesin fired again, but the blast of the sunfire rifle slapped against the daemon and dissipated without doing any damage. The daemon grinned, revealing half a dozen serrated fangs. It beckoned to them, running a claw down its lithe body, long tongue sliding suggestively over its teeth. Maesin unleashed another bolt from the sunfire with no apparent effect.

The daemon's face twisted into a savage grimace and it bounded forward, fast on bird-like legs, covering the ground before Illiathin could react. Tethesis moved first, swinging the carbine like a club, smashing the butt of the weapon into the side of the daemon's head.

The other daemon broke free from its body-wrapping, shedding the skin with a shudder and an expression of ecstasy. Illiathin fired out of pure instinct, the ball of charged particles from his gun flashing past the daemon's head.

Maesin and Tethesis were pounding the other daemon with their weapons, smashing its head and body, kicking and screaming incoherently in their terror. The creature writhed and howled, lashing out with claws and barbed tongue. Maesin fell back, her chest opened to reveal bloodied ribs sheared through by the daemon's claw.

Knowing it would not help but unable to do anything

else, Illiathin shot the daemon running towards him. The blast struck it square in the face, smearing its features like putty. It stumbled back, wailing in pain from a mouth that had slid down to its neck, its eyes obliterated.

Illiathin spared a glance at his brother. Tethesis stood over the remains of the other daemon, which resembled a bloodied bag of parts more than a humanoid creature. It spasmed, claws snapping, jaw mouthing silent threats.

The distinctive noise of flesh sloughing away caused the brothers to turn.

Maesin stood behind them, her face split from right eye to top lip, her clothes and flesh falling away. Daemon magic pulsed in her chest where she had been wounded, silver liquid leaking from severed blood vessels.

Horrified, Illiathin stood immobile as the daemon-Maesin leapt, the tip of a newly emerged claw rasping across Tethesis's throat. His finger tightened on the trigger at the same moment, turning Maesin's head into an incinerated pulp.

Both fell to the ground, Tethesis pinned beneath the lifeless remains of daemon-Maesin. Illiathin saw that the route to the door was free of danger and the urge to run welled up in him. His brother was dead, or as good as, and there was nothing to be done, but some sense of duty snared Illiathin, causing him to remain.

He saw a glow from a pouch at his brother's belt, dark blue. Snatching it from the body, Illiathin found inside the gem he had given him. At his touch it pulsed with life, but the blue was darkening, polluted by a spreading blackness.

Looking at Tethesis, he realised that the stone was linked to him, and as his brother's features started to contort into those of a daemon, Illiathin knew what had to be done.

He fired a burst of shots from the carbine, disintegrating what remained of his brother's chest and head. The stone in Illiathin's other hand throbbed in his grasp, the light brightening, the darkness seeping away to leave a beautiful cobalt glow.

The daemons were recovering, their grunts and moans growing in volume. Illiathin looked at the body of his brother and knew that he was totally alone. He had killed the last friendly face he knew, and for all he could tell the rest of his long life would be spent alone in this terrifying realm.

Fear broke through the trance as claws scraped on the floor behind him. He dropped the sunfire and ran, not daring to look back.

27

Through his connection to her, Asurmen could feel the thoughts of Neridiath falling into turmoil. She could think of nothing except that moment of hopelessness she had felt with him as he had shared the circumstances of Tethesis's death. The utter lack of power, the knowing submission to fate had brought to her mind the incident in the storage bay. He now shared that memory, the sensation of his fingers at Manyia's throat, the sure and certain knowledge that he would have to kill his daughter.

It was shocking how close she had come, even when there were weapons to hand with which she could have defended herself. Fear had paralysed her, the same fear that drove her now, but it was not death that inflicted such dread. Something far deeper and more visceral than simple mortality influenced Neridiath's choices.

In the storage room she had been helpless, saved by the instincts of a frightened child and the petty mental defences of a human. Death, perhaps torture and degradation, the murder of her child, had been but a breath away from reality.

Let me help you, said Asurmen. He drew in more of Neridiath's spirit, allowing his own psychic potential to envelop her. He used the connection to create a facsimile existence, the two of them standing in a dark chamber facing each other. A single candle flickered on a stand between them.

As he had told his warriors before the confrontation with the Dark Lady, he needed no temple. He was the incarnation of the shrine, the embodiment of the peaceful repose before violent acts. He allowed Neridiath a moment to compose herself before speaking.

'Focus on what I say,' he told her. 'Let my words enter your thoughts freely. Do not analyse them. Do not trust or distrust them. Simply allow them to be. Can you do that?'

Neridiath nodded, uncertain at first but then with more vehemence.

'Yes, I can do that.'

'That is good. You are strong, very strong. Too strong. For a long time you have trodden the Path and dammed up emotions that are destructive. That is the purpose of the Path, to guard us against those extremes. Now the time has come to let go, to confront those feelings and thoughts. They are blinding you to a greater truth. They are binding your spirit to a fate it does not desire.'

Asurmen stepped closer to the candle and Neridiath looked up. Her eyes widened in surprise. Asurmen was clad not in his armour but in the form he had worn before the Fall. He was shorn of his wargear, of the legend that hung like a mantle about his shoulders. He was not Asurmen in that moment, he was Illiathin again.

'There is a fear within you, Neridiath. You avoid it, but you cannot hide it forever. You must look upon it and in doing so you will rob it of all power to control you. Remember. Remember the time the fear began. Do not think of it, but picture it, relive it.' He felt resistance from the pilot. His voice grew firmer. 'Listen to me! You must fight. You must break the hold this dread has upon you. The sake of our people depends upon it. Your daughter needs you to be strong.'

At the mention of Manyia, a succession of emotions crossed Neridiath's face. Grief at first, and then she was afraid. The fear turned to anger and she snarled at Asurmen.

'I will not let her see that! I will not become what my mother became!'

And there it was, the moment that had sown such dread in Neridiath. Asurmen latched onto it, burrowing his mind into hers, dragging free the suppressed memory.

She was young, but old enough to know her own mind. Her mother stood at the door, looking back at her. Neridiath emanated waves of love, mingled with desperate hope and pleading. From her mother came nothing. Cold eyes regarded her as nothing more than bones and meat. A sneer lingered on her mother's lips. Disdain, not love. The child's eyes were drawn to the rune marked upon her mother's brow. The symbol of the Fire Dragons writ in dried blood. She had never seen it before, always removed before her mother had left the shrine. It seemed a grotesque thing, an icon of anger and death.

Her mother stayed at the threshold for some time and Neridiath sobbed, hiding her face in her hands. She felt the hot wetness of her tears and a thought occurred to her. She raced towards her mother, hands outstretched, hoping to use her tears to wipe away that dreadful rune.

Neridiath's mother caught her wrist in one hand and twisted, throwing the child to the ground. It had been a moment of instinct, no intent to harm or hurt behind it. Rubbing her arm, Neridiath looked up and saw that there was no response from her mother. She seemed neither glad nor ashamed.

'Come away.' Neridiath turned at the sound of her older cousin's voice from the doorway behind her. She glanced back and saw Fasainarath standing with his hand held out to her. 'Come here, Neth, away from that thing.'

Thing. Her mother was a thing now. That thing had a name. She was dimly aware of it, spoken in whispers by her family and friends, acknowledged but never welcome.

Exarch.

Her mother was an exarch, driven to bloodshed and the worship of Khaine until she died. What she had been was lost. Now all that remained was the warrior.

Reeling, Asurmen broke his mind free of Neridiath's. He had encountered many exarchs in his long existence. Indeed he had been the first. But never before had he understood the transition, the effect it had on others. Seeing a spirit becoming trapped on the Path of the Warrior through Neridiath's eyes made him understand from whence her fear stemmed. This was the place she had returned to, cornered in the storage bay. Her thought had not been for herself but for Manyia, not her daughter's death but the loss of her innocence.

'You are not your mother,' he said firmly, stepping past the candle to lay a hand on her shoulder. He had assumed his warrior countenance again, clad in blue armour. The psyche-shrine became light around them, a bare white chamber in the centre of his mind. 'Very few that tread the Warrior's Road become trapped. You are stronger than she was.'

'What if I like it? The killing?'

'You will,' Asurmen told her. The truth could not be avoided. 'You cannot fight that. You will feel triumph and dismay in equal weight. You will desire thrill of battle, the rush of blood. These are things that we cannot deny about ourselves. I will teach you how to control them, how to harness the incredible powers that our bodies have been gifted by our ancestors. You will become the weapon and you will learn to draw the war mask so that the shame and the hunger can be kept at bay, unleashed like a beast when necessary, caged when not needed. That beast lurks within you, unfettered, ready to burst free. You are a danger to your daughter if you do not learn how to handle it.'

'But I have to fight *now*. You want me to attack those ships. I can't... I can't lose Manyia. What if she senses my bloodlust. I won't defile her!'

'You have to fight.' Asurmen's voice became an insistent growl. 'You have only irrational fear to conquer. The threat is real, your dread is not. You can break the fear, but only if you try. Now you have the opportunity to prove to yourself that you are not a monster. Use it!'

She had a weapon, as much as if she had a knife or pistol in hand. She was the *Patient Lightning* and the ship's warlike creed seeped into her thoughts, provoking her, telling her that there was nothing to fear. She did not fight the desire. She embraced it. She had chosen to be powerless, but that had simply been the choice to be a victim.

Neridiath recognised that what she wanted more than anything else was revenge.

She felt tainted, broken by the realisation, but it did not make the desire go away. It was a part of who she was, a seed sown by recent events. She could allow it to become a cancerous growth, poisoning her thoughts, driving a rift between her and her daughter, or she could accept that she was not perfect, in thought or philosophy.

'I don't know how to fight,' Neridiath murmured, but even as the thought occurred she realised it was not true. She was part of the *Patient Lightning* and the battleship had been fighting for longer than its pilot had been alive.

She opened herself up to the starship, letting herself become its consciousness, the mortal link needed for its immortal spirits.

28

Asurmen watched as the battleship slowed and turned, twisting through a curving course to bring the forward batteries to bear on the closest Shard. The holofields activated, turning the sleek warship into a fractured cloud of light and conflicting sensor returns. The Chaos ships tried to adjust for the battleship's sudden change of tactic, but they could not match the manoeuvrability of the eldar vessel.

The targeted ship opened fire, lashing out towards the *Patient Lightning*'s last position with a flurry of shells and laser beams. Their woeful firing went far adrift, targeting systems sent awry by the dislocating effect of the holofields. Unscathed, the battleship pounced on its prey and unleashed the full strength of its forward turrets. Red energy lanced across the void, striking the Shard close to its centre. It possessed no protective shields and split almost immediately, the strange surface of the hull blistering like scorched skin. Debris and burning gas flared from the gash torn into its flank, explosive decompression hurling hundreds of charred bodies into the void.

Asurmen was still in psychic contact with Neridiath and allowed her feelings to pour into him. Together they felt like shouting and singing and crying, all at the same time. She knew that this was the delight that had scared her so much, but the fear had been erased by the desire for vengeance. Asurmen assured her he was proof that the pain, the anger and the hatred could be mastered, but not if they remained hidden. The pilot allowed the joy of killing to wash through her, and from her it swept through the *Patient Lightning*'s matrix.

Buoyed by her enthusiasm the battleship turned gently, the weapons systems down its right flank rippling volleys of plasma and missiles into the stricken Chaos vessel as the *Patient Lightning* circled the doomed ship. Explosions tore chunks of armour from the superstructure, stone-like material breaking away in jagged fragments that looked strangely like the Shards themselves, as they too had once been a piece of something far larger.

The path to open space was clear and for a moment it looked as if Neridiath would head for the gap. Asurmen was sure that all three Shards had to be destroyed. He used the memory of Tethesis's death, seizing hold of the pilot's thoughts of freedom, dragging her back to that moment in the storage bay, the terrifying vulnerability she had felt when her mother had left for the last time. She stood on the brink of the abyss and stared into it again.

Bring out that darkness against those that trapped you, Asurmen told Neridiath. *Find strength in the weakness, purpose in the fear. Master the anger, do not flee from it.*

Her focus returned to the remaining Chaos ships. Sharing her determination, the *Patient Lightning* headed back towards orbit, picking up speed. Beside the battleship swooped *Stormlance*, the much smaller ship's weapons bristling with power, evidence of the starship's growing excitement.

Neridiath plunged the *Patient Lightning* directly towards the two remaining Shards, guided by the instincts of the battleship's matrix.

More fire erupted as the enemy tried to target the incoming eldar vessels. A few lucky shots impacted on the battleship's hull. Wildly veering missiles passed under the *Patient Lightning* while hundreds of unguided rockets exploded uselessly behind *Stormlance*. Asurmen shared the sensation of the diffraction of the holofields increasing as the *Patient Lightning* continued to pick up speed, the erratic fire of the enemy becoming even more inaccurate.

The two eldar detected the same malign intelligence they had felt when they had first arrived in the star system. The Chaos ships were not wholly things of material and mechanics, but fashioned from some stranger substance that possessed a life, a desire of its own.

The remaining two Shards took up position abeam of each other, slowing down as they poured energy from their strange reactors into their sensor screens, desperately sweeping the nearby void for a solid sign of the eldar vessels. Asurmen felt probing lasers and radiation waves scattering from *Stormlance*'s holofield like rain on a glass canopy. Still blinded, the other ships approached cautiously, keeping close together in the hope that their overlapping fire would deter their foes.

Neridiath steered a course directly for the gap between the two Chaos vessels, absorbing the wisdom from the ship that they were as likely to hit each other as they were the *Patient Lightning* if they opened fire while the battleship passed between them.

The eldar gunners directed the remaining power coursing through the matrix to the front lances, unleashing a blistering salvo of energy bolts into the closest enemy ship.

Asurmen watched with satisfaction as the hull of the ship cracked along its length, the flicker of human lives within fading quickly as air escaped into the freezing vacuum of space. Neridiath shared the moment with him, relishing the accomplishment.

The Shard was not wholly crippled and returned fire. Dorsal turrets spewed out a torrent of explosive shells that threw immense hunks of shrapnel and secondary explosives onto the closest solar wing of the battleship. The golden sail shredded and the mast split, splinters of wraithbone skeleton and outer housing scattering into the void.

Stormlance darted ahead, its weapons discharging a torrent of laser fire into the already damaged ship, opening up further welts in the outer hull. The salvo obliterated weapons turrets studding the outer hull as it sped along the flank of the Shard. Another burst of fire from its keel turret sliced through the engines, setting off a succession of explosions that culminated in a spectacular reactor breach. A plume of superheated gas fountained as blue fire into the darkness and arcs of leaping electricity coruscated across the remnants of the ship as they spun away from each other.

To Neridiath the damage to the mainmast felt as though someone had stabbed a knife into her lower back, piercing the spine. Asurmen felt the same through their psychic link, though much reduced. The battleship pilot suppressed a groan and compensated for the loss of power, sliding the *Patient Lightning* towards the last Chaos vessel. The gunners siphoned as much energy as they could into the right-flank batteries, powering up the shorter-ranged but more powerful sunstorm batteries. A tempest of crackling plasma erupted from the battleship's flank as it moved past the Shard, the enemy ship's decks buckling as the stream of star matter slammed through its ebon hull.

The lance turrets added their strength, beams of red carving apart the Chaos vessel, turning stone-like matter into glittering dust and burning vapour. Looping over the battleship, *Stormlance* raked the exposed innards of the ship with more laser fire, cutting through support spars and armoured bulkheads so that the centre of the ship collapsed under its own artificial gravity field.

Almost unexpectedly, the last Shard broke apart into three tumbling pieces of wreckage. His instincts dulled slightly by Neridiath's combined psyche, it took a few moments for Asurmen to realise that the battle was over. Relief more than any other emotion surged through the Phoenix Lord.

With the three Chaos vessels destroyed, Neridiath's thirst for death started to abate, but the *Patient Lightning* was not yet done. From the spirits of the ship welled the desire to strike back at the weapons platforms that had forced the battleship to crash. Giving in to the vessel's desire, Neridiath guided the ship down to lower orbit.

Aware of the danger posed by the orbiting forts – five of them had been reactivated by the Chaos followers – the eldar vessel easily avoided their salvoes of torpedoes and missiles. *Patient Lightning* and *Stormlance* made short work of the stationary weapons satellites, cutting them apart with brisk lance fire, the shattered remnants left to spiral down and burn up in the atmosphere.

29

The battle was over, leaving Neridiath feeling cold and numb. She disconnected from the battleship's systems and almost fell out of the piloting cradle. Her legs weak, her heart hammering, she toppled to her knees on the deck of the command capsule, unable to stop her body shaking.

She felt disgusted, at herself and what she had done. The memory of the happiness the deaths of her enemies brought her flooded back, but she could recognise the bitterness behind it. She sensed Hylandris standing close at hand, but dared not look up, afraid of what she would feel when she saw Manyia. Her daughter had lashed out in infantile ignorance, but Neridiath had just murdered thousands of humans in cold blood. What message was that for her daughter?

'We fight or we die,' Hylandris said, laying a hand on her shoulder. Neridiath shrugged it off but he placed it again, squeezing reassuringly. 'It is the legacy the past has left for our people. We do not have the luxury of inactivity, or we would become casual observers of our own doom, as we were before.'

Neridiath stood up, grimacing, and took Manyia from him. The child was asleep still, oblivious to everything that had happened, unknowing of her mother's strife. Untainted, thought the pilot, and the realisation brought tears of relief.

'What happens now?' she asked. 'What do I have to do?'

'I do not know, but you are not the first to feel this way, and will not be the last. The Path exists for us to manage these emotions so that they can no longer destroy us.'

'I have to become an Aspect Warrior?' she asked, the horror of the thought almost choking the words in her throat.

'Yes,' said Hylandris, moving his hand from her shoulder to Manyia. 'For her sake, you must move onto the next stage of the Path. In time it will bring solace and you will become closer to your daughter without the burden of fear hanging on your spirit. You have to banish your anguish in the temples of Khaine. I know that if there is any being that can tell you the truth of this, it is Asurmen.'

'I need to go,' Neridiath said. 'I have to rest. I have to think.'

'Thank you,' said Hylandris. He stepped back and took off his ghosthelm, revealing a slender, ageing face. He had dark brown eyes, surprisingly kind. 'For acting when you were called upon. With the *Ankathalamon* in our possession, we can save Anuiven. Do not forget that, and know your pain is not without meaning.'

XIV

'There's nothing here,' said Jain Zar as they walked down the ramp of the ship.

'Air, food, shelter,' said Asurmen. 'What else do you need?'

He had tried to find somewhere not tainted by the Fall and it had taken much journeying to find the empty moon colony. All of the essentials – the bio-garden, the atmosphere processors, the psychic circuit – had been grown, but the populace had not yet arrived when the catastrophe had occurred.

'Something to do?' Jain Zar suggested.

'Do?' Asurmen led his companion from the docking area into the first hab-pod. 'There is plenty to do. We have to learn how to make weapons, armour, and how to use them. You must discover the means to control your instincts, to channel your rage into a useful purpose. We have food to grow, like-minded survivors to find. We *have a shrine to build, the first in a thousand generations. Things to do will not be in short supply.'*

'What is this place, anyway?'

'The birthplace of a new regime. Its name is unimportant.'

'You're wrong. Names are important. Names shape our expectations, give form to ideas. It should have a good name if you want to bring others here. A name that promises hope.'

'Asur. The silence, the heart, the wisdom at the centre of the universe. How about that as a name?'

'Asur? Yes, that will be very good. And what is this shrine? A temple of Asuryan?'

'No, Asuryan has guided me here and will continue to guide me, but there is another god whom we must call upon in these dark times.' Asurmen paced around the circular chamber. 'Here will be its beating heart, and about it we will build dormitories and armouries and chambers of reflection and contemplation.'

'You sound eager, but that is a lot of work for two of us,' said Jain Zar.

'I shall teach you what I have learnt. We will find others and teach them. They will find others in turn and teach them, and so the future will come into being as we shape it.'

'To rebuild our civilisation?'

'No, that is lost. We do not deserve another empire. We do what we must to survive, to endure long enough that we might fight back against the foe that has laid us low. We shall be the nemesis of Chaos, and though it will destroy us we shall be its destruction also.'

Jain Zar circled the room, thoughtful.

'A shrine to another god. Which one?'

'The god of our bloody passions, the lord of war, the deathbringer,' said Asurmen. 'Let me tell you of Khaine the Bloody-handed.'

30

Asurmen stood with Hylandris and watched Neridiath board *Stormlance*. Across the cavernous docking bay the stars shimmered in the open portal, the void kept at bay behind an invisible force field. Asurmen felt smug satisfaction emanating from the farseer.

'You are pleased with this conclusion of events?' the Phoenix Lord asked.

'It is as I have foreseen,' the seer replied. 'We leave this world with a victory. The *Ankathalamon* is in my possession and the machinations of Ulthwé will be curtailed. Anuiven need not die.'

'You foresaw this moment?'

Hylandris shifted from one foot to the other and back, uncomfortable with the question.

'Not this precise moment, I admit. I did not see your involvement at first. But that is the nature of prophecy, the skein does not rest, it is ever-changing.'

'Indeed it is. And yet the skein bends to my path, it

does not dictate it. I lead and others follow. One action can spawn a thousand fates for mortals, but my course is determined by my actions alone. There are few that can discern every future and chart the correct course.'

'It is the burden of the farseer that we must walk that narrow road, but my convictions have been proven correct.'

'In a sense. Even though you are driven by condescension for Anuiven, you yet desire the craftworld's forgiveness and acceptance. I speak not of your vision, which has been blinded for a long time by your arrogance and wish to assume the role of your craftworld's saviour in the hope of an impossible atonement. If the *Ankathalamon* was the only concern, I would have come here on my own and taken you and the artefact away from the danger. That was not my purpose in coming.'

The farseer stepped back, a scowl wrinkling his brow.

'I cannot see what other reason you have for aiding us, since the claiming of the *Ankathalamon* and the subsequent attack on Ulthwé has been my intent all along. I misled Zarathuin and the others but I cannot mask my plans from the skein itself. If, as you say, Asuryan guided you here it is to see my plan fulfilled.'

'I cannot say for sure what the outcome will be, that is not how the visions of Asuryan are employed. I saw only my part to be played, to destroy the vessels of the Chaos host. What happens next, I do not know. But I have come to understand that you cannot compete with the foresight of Eldrad Ulthran. You may think you have gained the advantage but it will not be so.' Asurmen looked down at the farseer, fixing him with a stare that Hylandris could feel even through the lenses of the Phoenix

Lord's helm. 'I also know that when the Rhana Dandra comes, our people will need Ulthwé more than Anuiven.'

'You think...' Hylandris seemed too horrified to voice his thoughts. He shook his head in denial. 'No, I cannot believe that you have helped me only to further Anuiven's destruction. You would not toss aside the fate of a whole craftworld so easily.'

'I seek the destruction of nothing, and I did not say that Anuiven must perish. I do not know what part the others of the Asuryata will play or have played in this game of fates. It is a sad state, an impossible choice, when one craftworld must die for another to survive. I will not choose sides, but act only as I have been shown. It is possible that none of us will understand until the Rhana Dandra comes.'

Asurmen walked away and started up the ramp to *Stormlance*.

'Wait!' Hylandris's desperate call caused the Phoenix Lord to turn. 'There must be something I can do to save Anuiven. What if I do not use the *Ankathalamon*? What if that is the threat that Eldrad saw and sought to prevent? I can choose not to act, can't I? Our destruction need not happen?'

'Perhaps, perhaps not. It may be too late. Events have been set in motion.' Asurmen turned and strode into *Stormlance*. Neridiath was waiting inside, and had evidently heard the exchange.

'Is it true? Will Anuiven perish?' She hugged her daughter tighter, fear in her eyes.

'I would not labour too many thoughts in concern for what may or may not come to pass. You have more pressing lessons that will demand all of your resolve.

When farseers play as gods there is no telling what the future holds.' Asurmen laid his hand on the pommel of his sheathed blade. The blue spirit stone fixed there flickered into life at his touch. 'But know this. No fate is final, not even death.'

ABOUT THE AUTHOR

Gav Thorpe is the author of the Horus Heresy novels *Deliverance Lost* and *Angels of Caliban,* as well as the novellas *Corax: Soulforge, Ravenlord* and *The Lion,* which formed part of the *New York Times* bestselling collection *The Primarchs.* He is particularly well-known for his Dark Angels stories, including the Legacy of Caliban series. His Warhammer 40,000 repertoire further includes the Path of the Eldar series, The Beast Arises novel *The Emperor Expects,* the Horus Heresy audio dramas *Raven's Flight, Honour to the Dead* and *Raptor* and a multiplicity of short stories. For Warhammer, Gav has penned the Time of Legends trilogy The Sundering, and much more besides. He lives and works in Nottingham.

THE CHAPTER'S DUE

GRAHAM McNEILL